The Lost Princes of Ambria
Royal fathers in search of brides!

Come to the breathtaking land of Ambria and get swept up in Raye Morgan's captivating world of feel-good fantasy as you fall in love with three royal daddies who juggle duty, fatherhood—and finding their perfect wives!

SECRET PRINCE, INSTANT DADDY!
November 2010

SINGLE FATHER, SURPRISE PRINCE!
December 2010

CROWN PRINCE, PREGNANT BRIDE!
January 2011

THE RELUCTANT PRINCESS
January 2012

PREGNANT WITH THE PRINCE'S CHILD
March 2012

Dear Reader,

As the song says, memories light the corners of our minds. Memory builds the structure of our lives, brick by brick, each representing happiness or regret or sadness or pride. It fills our thoughts with a rich background we wouldn't have without memory. But what if you lost yours?

Mykal Marten has lost his. He can't remember anything about Janis Davos, the woman he fell in love with two years before. That leaves Janis with a very big problem. How can you make up with a man who doesn't remember the terrible fight that tore you apart? How can you heal the wounds if one person doesn't know he's bleeding?

Her first impulse is to leave him behind and close off her memories. But one thing after another stops her, and soon she is trapped in a one-sided relationship. She loves him; he doesn't know who she is.

And that sets up an interesting experiment. Will he fall in love with her again? Was it just an accident of time and place, or is there something fundamental and important pulling them together? Are they made for each other? Is their love inevitable? Or will it crumble into ashes without those shared memories?

All this must play out against the excitement of Mykal being recognized as one of the Lost Princes of Ambria. But that only makes things worse for Janis. With her family's criminal past, she knows she can never fit in at the castle. She decides to fade out of his life before he finds out she belongs there—and before he knows about the baby.

Hope you enjoy reading about Mykal and Janis.

All the best

Raye Morgan

RAYE MORGAN

Pregnant with the
Prince's Child

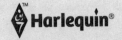

TORONTO NEW YORK LONDON
AMSTERDAM PARIS SYDNEY HAMBURG
STOCKHOLM ATHENS TOKYO MILAN MADRID
PRAGUE WARSAW BUDAPEST AUCKLAND

Recycling programs
for this product may
not exist in your area.

ISBN-13: 978-0-373-74163-2

PREGNANT WITH THE PRINCE'S CHILD

First North American Publication 2012

This edition published by arrangement with Harlequin Books S.A.

For questions and comments about the quality of this book please contact us at Customer_eCare@Harlequin.ca.

www.Harlequin.com

Printed in U.S.A.

Raye Morgan has been a nursery-school teacher, a travel agent, a clerk and a business editor, but her best job ever has been writing romances—and fostering romance in her own family at the same time. Current score: two boys married, two more to go. Raye has published more than seventy romances, and claims to have many more waiting in the wings. She lives in Southern California, with her husband and whichever son happens to be staying at home at the moment.

Books by Raye Morgan

Other titles by this author available in ebook format.

This book is dedicated to CB—which could stand for Clearly Beloved.

CHAPTER ONE

"Look."

Mykal Marten held out his cupped hands and opened them slowly. Perched on his palm was the most stunning butterfly Janis Davos had ever seen. Its lacy wings sparkled pink and silver as they pulsed in the sunlight.

"Be careful," she cried without thinking. "Don't hurt it."

He gave her a quizzical look, as though wondering why her first thought might be that one. "I would never hurt it," he said, his voice low and rough with emotion. "I just wanted you to see it. It's so beautiful, so precious...." His voice went so soft she could barely hear his words. "It reminds me of you."

She turned to look up into his crystal blue eyes, her heart in her throat.

"Oh, Mykal," she whispered, tears threatening. She looked more deeply into his eyes, hoping for truth. Did he really mean it? About her? There had been so many lies in her life, she was almost afraid to believe. And then she laughed with happiness.

Her laugh must have startled the butterfly, because it took off, circling above them, rising higher and higher in the offshore breeze, until it was just a sparkle against the blue sky.

They watched until it disappeared, and then she tucked herself into the crook of his arm and sighed.

"Here's the truth, Mykal. That butterfly was my heart. You set it free." She looked up, searching his eyes, hoping to see that he felt like she did, almost afraid that he wouldn't. "I never knew life could be like this," she said simply.

He pulled her in closer, wrapping her in his strong arms and smiling down into her face. "Neither did I," he said softly. "I never knew what love was until there was you."

He kissed her lips slowly, touching her tongue with his, savoring every nuance of her taste. "Promise me we'll never let it slip through our fingers, like other people do," he murmured. "Promise me we'll always re-member this day and how we felt."

"I promise," she said, reaching up to get more of his kisses. "And what's more, I prom-ise it will only get better."

Only get better. Only get better.

Her own words echoed mockingly in her head no matter how hard she tried to blot them out. That was then. This was now. How did you celebrate the death of a romance?

You didn't. You just tried to survive it.

And now, here she was in front of Mykal's family home, ready to sign, seal and deliver an official end to all they had meant to each other only months ago. She shifted the satchel she was carrying and wrapped her fingers around the beautifully twisted bars of the wrought-iron fence that topped the limestone wall that held back those who didn't belong inside.

Of course that meant her. Especially her.

Blame it on the war. Everybody else did. She'd used that excuse herself when she'd married Mykal, a man she'd known at the time for less than two months. Their marriage had been passionate, intense, and only lasted for a few weeks before their separation. All in all, it hadn't quite been half a year since they'd first met, though it seemed a lifetime. Blame it on the war. A whole generation of young Ambrians had given in to impulses they never would have thought of before the war drums had begun to beat a rhythm to their lives.

She and Mykal had both volunteered for military intelligence work, both taken some very tough training, and when they met later on as the war was ending, they'd seemed to be so well matched, she found it hard to believe that the man she'd married could have possibly grown up in this…well, it was a mansion, wasn't it? There was no way to put a more modest face on it. Rich people lived here. Very rich people.

She and Mykal had never talked much about their backgrounds. She hadn't realized he was hiding his just as surely as she had been hiding hers. She'd been pretty sure he didn't secretly have a family in organized crime like she did. But then, she didn't talk to anyone but her brother Rolo about that.

And here she was, standing outside of the address where she'd been told he now lived, trying to get up the nerve to go to the door and ask to see him. She didn't belong here. Her heart was beating a wild salsa in her soul and her knees felt like water. She was scared stiff.

But what she was most afraid of was her own traitorous heart. Would she let him walk all over her emotions again? Would she be able to keep the cold, sharp edge of her bitterness alive once she looked into his mesmerizing blue eyes?

She had to. She wasn't just building a life for one any longer. She couldn't afford to follow her heart. Two months in a prison camp had taught her to stop dreaming and start facing reality. That tended to happen when the man you thought was the love of your life turned you over to the secret police.

She looked at the brass bell meant for visitors to announce their business. What was she going to say to the butler? She had to get in to see Mykal one last time.

Mykal. It still took her breath away to think of him, and she had to control that. He didn't love her anymore. That much was perfectly clear. But she needed his signature on a couple of official documents. And then they could cut the last ties between them and walk away and never look back.

Her hands were trembling. Could she hold it together long enough to get all that done? She had to.

The street was empty. Clumps of grey snow lingered in the shadows. It was almost twilight. It had been a long, hard journey to get here and she'd hurried to make it before dark.

"So, what now?" she murmured to herself. "Shall I ring? And if they say, 'No visitors', then what? Do I make a scene? What do I do?"

Suddenly, a medical van turned onto the street, siren blaring. Janis jumped back, stepping behind a bush. She knew it was coming right for this house. Somehow, she knew. And as it turned in, the iron gates began to open.

Despite everything, she was still quick and resourceful. She didn't know if the van was bringing someone in or taking someone away, but she did know this might be her only chance to get onto the property without anyone challenging her. Trying to stay inconspicuous, she held the satchel with her papers close and slipped in through the gates alongside the van, staying well away from where the big side mirrors could pick her up. She was still wearing the dark blue jump-suit they'd made her wear in the prison camp and now she was glad for it. Anyone looking out and seeing her would assume she was in uniform and working with the medical van. This way she would have a chance of finding Mykal before someone kicked her out.

The van turned and pulled slowly into place, backing toward the wide stairway. A serving person had opened the double doors to the house and was on his way down the stairs toward the van. She went the opposite direction and seemed to escape notice, as all attention was on the van as the door opened and a paramedic jumped out, shouting orders forward to the driver.

She was almost in when a voice stopped her.

"Hey."

She gasped and looked up. A medic was looking down out of the ambulance at her.

"Hey, miss," he said. "Can you make sure they're ready for him inside?"

"Oh." She almost laughed with relief. "Sure. No problem."

"Thanks."

That answered that question. This was a delivery, not a pickup. There had to be a lot of people living in a house this big.

A few more steps and she was inside, giving only a quick glance at the beautifully appointed foyer and the sweeping stairway to the second floor. She had to figure out how to find Mykal and in a house this size, that wasn't going to be easy.

"Yes? Can I help you?"

"Oh!"

She whirled and faced an imposing-looking gentleman in formal wear. She was caught. She had to think fast. She wasn't sure just exactly what was going on, so it was difficult to make adjustments. She needed a story that would fit in. Luckily, her military intelligence training had been thorough and it kicked in now.

"I came in with the medevac van," she said, careful not to do any actual lying. She glanced out at where the van had backed up to the front stairway. The double doors were open and someone was being unloaded on a gurney. She looked again, gaze sharpening. There was a man...and he looked familiar.

Her heart stopped and she reeled.

The man on the gurney was Mykal.

Mykal! her mind screamed, and for a split second, everything went black. Mykal was hurt. All the love, all the feeling came pouring back. The anger, the pain, the betrayal—all that disappeared in a puff of smoke. Mykal was hurt. Everything in her demanded she go to him.

But she couldn't. She saw his head move. He even nodded in answer to something one of the paramedics said to him. Relief filled her heart. At least he wasn't unconscious.

But what was he? Wounded? Ill? She couldn't tell. But she knew what her plan had to be. It came to her very clearly in a lightning-quick flash. To people in the house, she had to appear to be with the medevac team. To the medevac team, she had to appear to belong at the house. Mykal was hurt and she knew she had to pretend she didn't know him for now. Until she had a chance to see him alone, she couldn't let anyone know who she was or why she was here. For all she knew, there might be standing orders to keep her away.

It would be more than tricky, because she needed to stay out of Mykal's line of sight at the same time. If he looked up and saw her…

All of that thought process transpired in a fraction of a second. As she knew from her training, acting like you belong there and you know what you're doing is half the battle. She turned back to the butler and managed to put on a professional smile.

"If you could direct me to the room he'll be using, I'd like to check it out and make sure the accommodations will suit his needs."

The man hesitated a moment and she thought she could detect just a hint of suspicion in his eyes. But he didn't say anything. Instead, he stood back and gave her a gracious bow of welcome, then turned and led her past the sweeping curve of the huge staircase to a room at the back of the house.

"We decided to prepare the extra bedroom here on the first floor rather than his usual suite so that the stairs could be avoided for now," he told her, and she nodded her approval of that decision after a quick look inside. But his words also made her wonder—was he in a wheelchair? Was he paralyzed? Each thought made her quiver inside.

"It looks fine," she said, noting there was a bathroom attached. All in all, it was larger and nicer than any apartment she'd ever had in her life and it was just a spare room. "I'm sure we will be able to make him comfortable here."

There was a shout from one of the technicians escorting Mykal in and she noted it with a gesture. "Please don't feel you have to stay with me," she said. "I think the medical team might need some guidance right now."

"Of course." He gave her a quizzical look, but he did as she suggested, and she sighed, sinking like a sack of rocks onto the bed, her head in her hands. This was outrageous, as complex as any undercover assignment she'd ever had. She should be laughing—at herself for doing this, at anyone who took her seriously.

Mykal was hurt in some way but she couldn't

think about that. All she needed right now was a measure of time to talk to him before someone ordered her off the premises. And she knew very well that someone might end up being Mykal himself.

She closed her eyes for a moment, trying to center herself. This had seemed so simple. Her anger at Mykal had been simmering for a long time and she had planned to find him, glare right into his face and let him have it. She'd been all primed and ready, so filled with pain and resentment that she'd been sure she could pull it off. But she hadn't counted on him being hurt.

Mykal didn't get hurt. She'd shared enough espionage adventures with him to know that. He was like a golden child, unique and untouchable. Magic happened when he went undercover. Safes opened to reveal their bounty at his touch. Women swooned and gave away their deepest secrets. He smiled and doors opened. But he didn't get caught and he didn't get hurt. Others did, but not Mykal. Those were the rules. It left her shaken to know someone had breached them.

She heard the paramedics coming down

the hall and she stood back as they brought him into the room, skimming the shadows, trying to stay out of his line of vision as long as she could. Luckily, the butler didn't come in with them so she only had to play one part of this multiple-sided game. So far, the paramedics were focused on their job and hadn't seemed to notice her beyond an original nod as they entered.

She didn't let herself really look at Mykal. She was afraid of what she might see and of the emotional response she might have. All of that had to be saved for later…if there was a later.

And then he spoke to her.

"Hey. Could you get me some water?"

The voice was rough, strained. He was obviously in a lot of pain. She looked up, meeting his eyes for just a second before they closed.

"Sure," she said, her heart thudding against the walls of her chest so hard she was sure everyone could hear it. "I'll get some right away."

He hadn't realized who she was. But she couldn't keep herself from staring at that face she'd loved so deeply. Despite the obvious ravages of his injuries, he was still as gorgeous as ever. She had to rip her gaze away, afraid she would be hypnotized by his beauty if she didn't take care.

She drew in a sharp breath, set her satchel down in a corner and slipped out of the room before he looked again, feeling very, very lucky. He wasn't totally himself and she hated to see him in this condition. But at least he hadn't realized who she was. She could breathe easy for a few more minutes.

Actually, being sent on this errand was a good thing. She needed to reinforce the impression she belonged here. She walked toward where she assumed the kitchen and butler pantry must be. Sure enough, the man himself was taking a sip from a suspicious-looking bottle as she came through the door. He put it away hurriedly and cleared his throat, trying to put the best face on it.

She smiled. More good luck like this definitely made her feel more secure and she waved away his apologetic look.

"We're getting him settled," she told him, attempting an air of professional courtesy.

"But we'd like to have a tray with a pitcher of water and a glass available for him at bedside. We've got something in the truck I can use, but I thought something he was familiar with using here at home would feel more comfortable for him."

"Of course, miss." He began to set one up for her right away. "My name is Griswold, by the way. I'm in service until nine tonight. After that, it's just the night watchman, but you can dial the nine on the phone and you'll get him." He handed her the tray. "Here you are. Would you like me to…?"

"No, I'll take it myself. Thank you so much."

She started off but he called to her.

"Miss…"

She turned back, her heart in her throat. Had he noticed something?

"Yes?"

He frowned at her for a moment and she held her breath. Then he shrugged and asked, "What kind of food shall I tell cook he will be needing?"

She bit her lower lip, trying to look thoughtful but panicking just a little bit. How the heck did she know? She didn't even know exactly what was wrong with him.

"I'll have to look at my instructions," she said quickly, "and get back to you on that. But I would assume it would be the usual light, bland sort of things."

Ouch, that sounded lame, didn't it?

"To start, I would prepare some chicken soup if I were you," she added quickly.

You could never go wrong with chicken soup. At least, she hoped not.

"Ah, yes. Thank you, miss."

"Of course." She nodded and left the room.

Once she was far enough from the kitchen, she paused and leaned against the wall, closing her eyes and catching her breath. What the heck was she doing, anyway? This had started out as a ploy to get close to Mykal without gatekeepers barring her way. But it was fast becoming something much more serious.

Funny. She'd spent the last few weeks in the prison camp going over everything she was going to say to him when she got out, again and again. It was how she'd kept herself sane. But now, the words were fading. Things weren't quite what she'd thought they would be.

Her emotions had run the gamut while she was imprisoned. She'd gone through sorrow, raging anger and finally, a deep, painful bitterness when she realized he really wasn't going to come and save her. No one was. She was lucky the camp had been liberated by the royal forces a few days before, or she would have been there still.

And Mykal—had he been here all that time, living like royalty, while she endured the horrors of the camp? Anger began to bubble up inside her again and she had to tamp it back. Anger got in the way of clear thinking and she would need her wits about her.

She was about to go back into his room. If he were dozing, she would have a chance of staying until the paramedics left. She wished she knew what had laid him low like this. An illness? A wound of some sort? She ached to know so that she could do something to help him.

But if he were wide awake, he would take one look, stare for a second, hardly believing she would have the nerve to show up here, and then probably order her out of his house and out of his life, just as he had the last time they'd been together.

She took a deep breath and steadied herself. In a moment, she would be alone with Mykal. That was what she'd come for, but when she came right down to it, that was really the scariest part of this.

CHAPTER TWO

"READY, set, go," Janis muttered to herself, her own private little pep talk.

She was about to face Mykal and make demands. She would be cool, calm and collected. She would remember her talking points. And she would be tough.

She'd never been very good at holding him to account. Their life together had been full of excitement, danger and fun. Neither one of them had ever insisted on guidelines. Neither of them had ever set out principles. Maybe that was what had doomed them from the start. When problems rose up between them, they had nothing to fall back on.

She hesitated outside the bedroom door, listening. They seemed to be finishing up, and in another moment, they were filing out the door.

The one with the curly red hair saw her first. "Oh, good. You've brought him water. I was going to go find some, but that will be better."

"We've settled him in," the dark-haired paramedic added, nodding as though he thought she was in charge here and he was making his report. "Have you been updated on his condition?"

She shook her head, maintaining a professional reserve. "No, I haven't. I'm hoping you can fill me in."

"Sure. Well, here's the deal. You probably know he was badly wounded when his motorcycle hit an IED a few weeks ago."

She didn't know. Emotions choked her throat, hitting her hard. She managed to hide it pretty well, but inside, she felt the trauma. The horror of picturing him in a motorcycle accident was almost too much to bear. But she couldn't show it. If she could control the trembling, she would be all right.

"He ended up with some broken bones, damage to a few internal organs, including possible brain damage, and shrapnel in his back. Most of the shrapnel was removed, but a few slivers are very close to his spinal cord. They haven't decided yet if they can risk going for them."

"Oh." Reaching out, she used the chair rail to keep herself upright, but he didn't seem to notice.

"We've got him braced pretty tightly. He won't like it when he fully wakes up. But you've got to keep him in it."

"Can he…" Her voice was choked and she had to clear her throat. "Can he walk? Is there paralysis?"

The paramedic hesitated. "So far, so good. But he has to be kept quiet. No physical activity. No major emotional upheaval." He shrugged. "I'm sure you know the drill."

"Do I?"

A wave of panic crashed over her. She couldn't help it. This was making her very nervous. She wasn't qualified for this. These people had the idea that she would take care of him. She wouldn't. She couldn't. What if she did something that injured him?

"I…I'm not experienced with spinal injuries," she stammered out. "Maybe you should call in someone who…"

He shook his head. "No need for that. Just keep him down as long as possible, that's my advice. That's why we've given him something to make him sleep. I left a couple of bottles of the medications prescribed for him and some other supplies on the shelf in the bathroom. The doctor will be coming in to see him tomorrow, about ten, so be ready for that."

"About ten," she repeated robotically, still stunned by what she was hearing.

"I left a list of the numbers to call if he needs anything." He shrugged. "But you seem to be pretty well staffed here. I don't suppose there will be any problems."

He gave her a half smile, as though he'd suddenly realized she was pretty. He shrugged. "He may be a little hard to handle. And he's got a wicked temper." He grinned. "But I guess that's understandable after all he's been through."

She blinked. That didn't sound much like the man she'd been married to. But she supposed things were different now. Then she remembered what he'd been like that last day, once he'd found out what she'd done. Yes, his temper had come out, cold and biting. *Wicked* hadn't been the word for it.

"Of course," she said weakly.

"And I guess that's it."

She nodded, not sure anymore if she was glad the medics were leaving. She'd wanted them to go before the butler came back, but now she wasn't so certain. Maybe he should have been here to hear all this. She bit her lip, not sure what to do, but they were leaving and what could she use as an excuse to stop them?

"Thank you so much for all your help," she said instead, feeling breathless. "Shall I show you the way out?"

"Don't bother, miss. We know the way." He gave her a grin. "See you again soon, I suppose. We'll be the ones to transport him to the castle when that comes up."

"Oh. Of course." She knew her smile was shaky but that couldn't be helped. "Goodbye." Then she watched as they made their way out. What could she say? She was completely bewildered.

It sounded as though his injuries had been life-threatening—and maybe still were. She felt as though she were taking a dive on a roller coaster every time she thought of that. Obviously, he might have died. Despite everything, she couldn't bear to think of it.

And the castle? Why on earth would he be going to the castle?

But that didn't matter. She had to get out of here.

Time to face facts: she'd been kidding herself. All this talk of tying up loose ends and coming to closure was a bunch of baloney. Deep in her heart, she'd been hoping for a confrontation, a knock-down drag-out that would curl Mykal's hair and set him back on his heels. She'd wanted him to know how he'd misjudged and hurt her. She'd wanted him to admit he'd been wrong to betray her. She wanted to throw his legendary self-confidence into disarray.

He wasn't always right. He'd been wrong. Very, very wrong.

But all that was impossible now. She couldn't confront him. He was in a precarious condition and had to be handled with kid gloves. It made her cringe to think of hurting him further. That confrontation she'd been so ready for would have to wait for another time.

She would have to go. There was no choice. She would go back to the kitchen and repeat everything the paramedics had told her, then tell the butler to take over Mykal's care himself.

How strange this all was. How frustrating.

With a deep, heart-felt sigh, she looked at the bedroom door. He was probably asleep by now. She might as well take in the water. It would give her a chance for one real look at him before she went.

She stopped, unsure. Should she risk it? She shrugged. What else could she do? Softly, she opened the doorway and slipped through it, her heart beating hard. Taking a deep breath, she entered the room and set the pitcher of water down before she looked at the bed.

Mykal's eyes were closed. It looked as if he were sound asleep. She swayed with relief, then took the opportunity to look at him more closely. Even though his face looked pale and drawn and there were dark circles under his eyes, he was as gorgeous as ever. Despite everything, her heart yearned for him. Was there any way to stop it?

No. She was just going to have to shove her feelings aside and learn to move on. She'd been tough before. Her whole life had been filled with hard choices, unpleasant consequences. She had to be totally tough now, and she knew she could do it. It wouldn't be easy. But she could do it.

But she was stalling and had to get away soon. Being this close to him again was hard. All the old feelings were still there, waiting to be released. And she had to make sure that didn't happen. He hadn't trusted her when she'd needed his support. He hadn't done anything to save her from the Granvilli secret police. Anyone with this sort of wealthy background surely should have had the influence to make things easier on her at least. But no help had come. That was something she would find hard to ever forgive.

Quickly, she went over in her mind exactly what she needed to get done. He had to sign the divorce papers she'd had drawn up. But most important—he had to sign away his parental rights to the child she was carrying.

That, she knew, might be the sticking point. That was the one she would really have to fight for.

Sighing, she turned and looked around the room. It was plain but elegant, decorated in white and gold. A flat-screen television sat on a table in one corner. A tall bookcase filled one wall. She walked over and began to study the titles, one by one.

She ought to go.

Now.

Well, in a minute.

Something deep inside was telling her that once she walked out the door, she might never be able to get this close to him again. Did she still love him? Her eyes filled with tears and she couldn't read the titles any longer.

"Hold it together," she told herself softly. "Just keep it calm."

But the sudden sound of a male voice made her jump and gasp at the same time.

"Looking for something?" he said.

She froze in sudden horror. The voice was Mykal's. There was no doubting it. She'd missed her chance to avoid this. Slowly, she turned, heart beating in her throat.

"Hello," she said, attempting a bright tone but achieving only a shaky rasp. Her version of a smile felt awkward. But she met his stunning blue-eyed gaze steadily. Like Anne Boleyn, she was ready to face the guillotine. "How've you been?"

"I've been better," he said, and grimaced.

She waited, hardly breathing, watching his eyes. The hair was standing up at the back of her neck. She expected fireworks. She expected he would call out her name, yell, shout, order her out.

Something. Some harsh emotion. But as she waited another second, and then another, her surprise began to grow. It wasn't happening. There was nothing.

The longer the silence lasted, the more breathless she became. Was he having trouble seeing in this dim light? Recognition should flash across his face any second now.

But his attention seemed to have drifted. Maybe it was the drug they'd given him. Maybe she could still slip out and...

Suddenly, he turned his gaze and looked at her penetratingly.

"Did my brother hire you?" he asked.

She stared at him, completely at sea. What was he talking about?

Mykal, she wanted to say. *It's me. Janis.*

But she couldn't say a thing. All she could do was stare at him. His eyes were just as blue as ever, just as beautiful, but nothing in there seemed to recognize her.

Was he playing a game with her? Torturing her in some creative new way? But no, he wasn't the type to do that, and anyway, he looked completely sincere. And what would be the point?

"Or did the castle send you over?" he went on, stretching back and closing his eyes. "I'll bet that's it."

What? The castle again. What was going on here?

"I...no, uh..." What could she say? She knew very well what she *should* say. She should tell him who she was and remind him of their past together. That was why she was here, wasn't it? But did she dare? Wouldn't that be inviting the very thing she had to avoid in order to keep him calm?

"I guess they thought I could use a day nurse," he muttered, sounding more irritable than friendly. "If they would just stop with the medication, I have a feeling I would do just fine without anybody's help."

She stood on the spot, paralyzed. He didn't seem to know who she was. But that was crazy. How could he forget? They were married, for heaven's sake. It might not have been a traditional sort of marriage, but it had been intense and wonderful while it lasted. Disappointing him had been a big mistake, and it had been ugly when he realized what she'd done. He'd lost all trust in her, and his response had broken her heart.

She looked at him, at the pale complexion, the short dark hair that curled about his head like a laurel wreath. He seemed very tired and as she gazed into the depths of his eyes, she could see that his injuries had done deep psychic damage along with the physical wounds. Soon, whatever the paramedic had given him would kick in and he would fall asleep. She had to leave.

But she hesitated. This was the man she had loved with all her heart and all her passion. This was the father of her coming child. How could he not see who she was?

Deliberately, she stepped into the light right in front of him. He looked surprised.

"Don't you know who I am?" she said, hating that her voice trembled as she spoke. "Don't you know why I'm here?"

He stared at her as though he were trying to see through a fog. "Sorry. Have we met before?"

She stared at him, frozen in wonder. Was she dreaming this? Searching his face, looking for answers, she had to conclude it was real. He was disgruntled, but there was no lurking animosity. And there was definitely no lurking recognition. He really didn't know who she was.

"If you were a nurse at the hospital, I really am sorry." He managed a crooked grin of boyish-looking apology. "I wasn't exactly a model patient at all times." He winced as though something hurt. "I guess I was pretty much out of it a lot of the time. I just might not have ever noticed you."

She half laughed, nervous and unsure. "I'm not a real nurse, you know," she said quickly. "I'm actually more of a…a…"

"A guard?" He nodded as though her puzzling behavior was finally becoming clear to him. "I understand. With these negotiations going on endlessly, I guess someone decided I might need extra protection. Especially considering the condition I'm in."

"Protection." She felt like a fool, parroting his words. But she needed something to give her a clue as to how she should act. She had no idea what negotiations he was talking about and the casual way he brought them up made her think they were somehow common knowledge—at least to anyone who had paid attention to the news and hadn't been wasting away in prison camp for weeks.

"Uh…what is your condition exactly?" she asked, knowing she might be opening a can of worms she wasn't going to be able to control, once opened. She wanted to hear from him just what he felt was damaging and dangerous—and why he didn't seem to remember things he should know by heart.

He grimaced, looking annoyed at the question. "Shrapnel from an IED. Most of it removed, but some slivers still close to the spine. Broken collarbone that's already mostly healed. Traumatic brain injury that doesn't seem to be as bad as they first thought." His voice took a bitter tone. "But either that, or the induced coma they put me in, seems to have wiped out a chunk of my life. Like, the last two years. Hope to get them back at some point." He looked at her wearily.

"You...you don't remember anything?"

"Nope. All gone."

She stared at him, speechless. He had amnesia? Their love, their marriage, the things he'd caught her doing—everything gone, like wiping a slate clean? She could hardly breathe. And she could hardly believe it was true.

His face darkened as he watched her reaction. "You're a funny sort of medical guard," he said, almost angry. "Where's your hard, Nurse Ratched attitude?"

Still stunned, she was having trouble working up anything coherent to say. She shook her head, blinking rapidly.

He made a gesture of disgust. "Listen, just go and leave me alone," he said, shifting against the pillows. "I really don't need anybody here. I'm okay. Just get out, why don't you...."

His voice broke and he gasped, turning to find relief from whatever was torturing him. She bit her lip. Obviously, the pain medication hadn't kicked in, or wasn't working. His eyes were closed and he was breathing unevenly.

She stared at him, still so beautiful, but with a line of bitterness around his mouth and a slow, smoldering sorrow that she'd noticed in his blue eyes. He looked like a man who'd had too much suffering and didn't want to have any more.

What had happened to him? What had made him lose his memory? And why didn't he respond to her the way she still responded to him? Had it all been a sham from the beginning? That thought made a bitter taste rise in her throat and she pushed it away.

He began to look better again. Whatever had been torturing him seemed to have weakened and she decided to attribute his bad attitude to pain and leave it at that. In another moment, he took a deep breath and straightened, looking almost normal.

"What shall I call you?" she asked as he blinked toward her in the light.

"Are you still here?" he asked, looking surprised. "I gave you every opportunity to go."

"I don't scare all that easily," she told him with a twisted smile. "What shall I call you?" she asked again.

"Mykal will do." He didn't smile back but he didn't look angry anymore. "If you really think you can handle it here, we might as well operate as though we were friends." A shadow passed over his eyes. "God knows it's going to be hard to find a friend soon. I'm afraid I'm being drawn into a world where such things can't last."

She had no idea what he was talking about, but she didn't ask.

"So what is the deal with your memory loss?" she said instead.

He gave her a mock wounded expression. "Do you know how hard it is to talk about something you can't remember?" He shifted his position carefully. "I lost over two years of my life. But it doesn't really bother me unless someone brings it up."

"Oh." She made a grimace of apology. "Sorry."

He grinned as though happy to be able

to set her back a bit. "No problem," he said. "Troublemaker," he muttered, just to tease her.

It warmed her, this back and forth. It was very like what they'd done together all the time in the old days.

"You don't wonder what you did?" she asked him. "All that time."

"I've been told what I did. At least, I've had a rough outline."

Sure, they'd probably told him about his military service, about working in intelligence. But had they told him about her? Had they told him he'd been married? Probably not. After all, very few people even knew. They'd kept it secret. If their commanding officers had found out, they would both have been expelled from the corps. Not even their friends had known about it. If she hadn't found the marriage license and her wedding ring in among her important things when they'd let her out of the prison camp, she might have begun to believe it was a fantasy herself.

"And?" she prodded.

"I guess I was in the military, but so far they

haven't been able to confirm that with the right agency. It seems I was doing some sort of undercover work or something. Very hush-hush. No one will admit anything. But I'm sure they will get paperwork squared away eventually. In the meantime, I'm a man without a past."

That was a pity. She had a big chunk of his past right here in her heart, but she couldn't hand it over. Not yet.

The pain came back in waves. She could see it as it came, read it in his eyes. He groaned softly and she could see that he was in real agony. Everything in her wanted to go to him, to help. But what could she do? She had no medical training. She was afraid anything she tried to do might only make him worse.

He groaned again, writhing, and she couldn't hold back any longer. She slipped into the bathroom, grabbed a washcloth and ran cold water over it, then hurried back and sat on the edge of his bed. For all she knew, this might be exactly the wrong thing to do, but she had to do something. Moving smoothly, she pressed the cool cloth to his forehead and began to murmur soft, soothing nonsense as she held it there. At any moment, she expected him to lash out at her, kick her away, yell something awful.

But to her surprise, he did none of that. Something in her touch seemed to calm him almost immediately. Little by little, his body began to relax.

"Do me a favor," he said suddenly, his voice choked. He was looking up at her with a strange expression on his face, as though he weren't sure how she was going to react to what he asked of her. "Could you hold my hand?"

She stared down at him, hardly breathing.

"I…I'm spinning," he explained gruffly as he reached out, closing his eyes again. "The medication. I just need… I don't know. To feel like I'm anchored to something."

She took his hand in hers and held it tightly, then pressed it to her heart. There was something so real, so vulnerable about the way he'd asked her, tears filled her eyes again and her throat choked with emotion.

This was so strange, a complete reversal of roles. Mykal was always the tough guy, the one whose arms she'd run to, the man who knew all the answers. And now here he was, asking her for reassurance. Asking for trust. For a solid center to cling to.

But she wasn't the one who could do that for him. Not now, not after all that had happened between them. Didn't he sense that?

"Mykal," she whispered, tears spilling over. "I…I can't…"

But he didn't hear her. He was already asleep.

She looked at the long, strong hand she was holding in both of hers. His beautiful hands had always been one of the things she'd loved best about him. She ached inside for what they'd had, what they'd lost. Bringing his hand up, she put it against her cheek and sighed. Then she kissed the center of his palm and laid it back down on his covers, letting her gaze run over every visible part of him. The light from the lamp made his skin glow and seemed to put every muscle in relief, like a beautiful landscape. Everything in her yearned to touch him. She'd missed him so much and hungered for this for far too long.

For just a moment she remembered the first time she'd met him.

She'd been sent to check out rumors of a commotion in a pub in the seaside town near where she'd been working. Walking into the room, she'd seen him and he'd filled her gaze like a star, brilliant and shining, the center of everything.

At first, she'd thought she'd caught him in the middle of a giant con. She knew he wasn't who he said he was and he knew she knew it. But it hadn't fazed him one bit. He'd given her a great big grin that told her everything she needed to know about him.

The war was already over at the time. The phony truce had begun, making things even more dangerous than they had been before. They were working in a border town filled with people who changed sides as easily as they changed their toothbrushes. Or maybe it just seemed that way as most people were busy playing both sides against the middle.

The little pub was filled with local officials scared to death their money-laundering scheme had been discovered by the Granvilli authorities. They were looking for a way out. Mykal had convinced them they were about to get caught and that they should let him hold the money for safekeeping. They were grateful as they turned the cash over to him. They even bought him drinks and made him the center of a general toast.

He loved what he was doing. He loved pulling the wool over their eyes and getting away with—well, not with murder exactly. But something pretty wrong at any rate. He took their money and left them feeling good about it. Sort of a modern day Robin Hood—if Robin Hood had been a spy for France.

And when she caught up with him outside the little pub and challenged him on it, he laughed. And then he picked her up out of sheer exuberance and twirled her around as though to the music still pumping out through the double doors of the place.

"You're right," he said. "And what are you going to do about it?"

She'd stared at him for a moment, then her lips twitched. He was completely adorable and impossibly mischievous at the same time. She was smitten. And she also knew she would never, ever forget him. So pretty quickly, she was laughing right back at him.

"Tell you what," she'd said. "I'll buy you a drink. But not here."

She wasn't all that surprised to find out they were both working for Granvilli Military Intelligence. Well, not exactly both. She was doing that, but he was doing something else as well.

He was a spy for the royal side. But she didn't learn about that until later. Still, she couldn't hold that against him. After all, she had some secrets of her own. And that was pretty much the heart and soul of the problem between them. Even when she'd thought he was deliciously devious, she hadn't understood just how convoluted his motives really were. And he still didn't know a lot about her.

The man she'd loved so passionately was still in there, somewhere. He needed her, even if he didn't realize what all that implied. There was no way she could leave until she knew he was safe.

With a sigh, she slumped down on the small couch that was set next to the bed. In another moment, she was curled into a ball and thinking protective thoughts. And then she was asleep herself.

* * *

Mykal woke carefully. He was doing every-thing carefully now. Even his dreams were tentative. Something was always warning him not to move. The excessive caution created a growing rage inside him, pure frustration. He wanted to shout and throw something. He wanted to punch something. He couldn't live the rest of his life this way.

Still, for now, he would be careful. The world around him seemed to be so full of changes, so many things happening to him and his future, so many things lost in his past, that he didn't want to risk making a wrong move. For now.

Lifting his head slightly, his gaze fell on a young woman curled up and sleeping on the couch next to his bed. It gave him a start but then he remembered who she was—someone the powers that be at the castle had sent over.

He didn't need her here. In fact, he resented it. He could take care of himself. Once this medication wore off, he would be okay. He would tell her to go back where she came from and leave him alone.

Still, he had to admit, he'd felt a tug of at-traction from the first. It was stronger now.

She was young and pretty with evidence of a lean, agile look to her nicely shaped body—though he couldn't see much of it under that shapeless jumpsuit of a uniform. Her sleek ash-blond hair fell over her cheek, shining like corn silk in the summer sunlight with a beauty that almost choked him for a moment. He hadn't had much beauty in his life lately. Suddenly, he had an overwhelming urge to reach out and touch it.

But he couldn't, he thought to himself sarcastically. He had to be careful. His groan was heartfelt and he shook his head. No, he wasn't going to be able to keep this up for long. There came a tipping point when life just wasn't worth living without a few common human activities. Touching a beautiful woman was one of them.

Currently he was clinging to optimism. Surely this would pass. He'd seen the X-rays. The pieces of shrapnel were mere slivers. How could such tiny things be so dangerous to his life? Maybe they would begin to move away or melt or…or something. And maybe his memory would come back and things would get back to normal.

He was blaming the amnesia on the fact that they had kept him in a drug-induced coma for weeks while they worried about a possible traumatic brain injury and debated what to do with the shrapnel. That ought to be enough to knock anybody's mind for a loop. He had no doubt the fog would clear away soon. But as for the shrapnel…

If he just could remember what exactly had happened. What had he been doing, what had he been thinking when he'd hit that IED? But it was gone—along with a few years of his life. He'd just lost it all. How did you do that? How did it happen? Whatever—it didn't make a lot of sense, but it seemed to be true that it had happened to him. And there was a deep, dark hole in his soul because of it.

The woman moved and murmured something in her sleep. It sounded like "get away from me," but it might have been something totally different. Still, it made him frown and wonder what was bothering her. He wanted to reach out and comfort her. And then he remembered. He couldn't do things like that anymore.

He grimaced.

Think about something else.

He looked around the room. His usual bedroom was upstairs, but he'd stayed in this one a time or two in his childhood—mostly when all the Swiss cousins had come to fill the house for the holidays. The furnishings had a nice heirloom look to them, although he knew his mother had worked hard to make bargains into antiques during their poverty-stricken period in his late teens. It was nice to be in a familiar place after all that time in the sterile rooms at the hospital.

He hadn't actually lived here since he'd gone away to university, more than ten years before. But he had a lot of childhood memories. It had been here on his eighteenth birthday that his parents had told him he was adopted. An admission like that was supposed to be a big shock in a young man's life, but as he remembered it, he had nodded thoughtfully, taking it in as something less than surprising.

He'd always known he was sort of an ugly duckling in the wrong nest—though most would have disputed the "ugly" appellation. His parents were nothing like him. All through his childhood they had watched him in a sort of state of awe, their mouths slightly open, as though they couldn't believe a child of theirs could act like that.

Not that they didn't adore him. If anything, they'd loved him a bit too much, to the point where his brother, Kylos, their natural-born son, felt as though he had to do ever more outrageous things in order to get noticed himself.

So once they had told him the truth, he felt vindicated in a way. That small, illusive memory sense deep inside that only came out in dreams to tell him something was deeply, horribly flawed inside him had it right after all. He was in the wrong family.

And now someone at the royal castle had decided he might be one of the lost princes who had scattered into hiding at the time of the original rebellion that overthrew the monarchy almost thirty years before. He had no idea if there was any truth to it. If there was, he wasn't so sure he wanted to participate. But his mind was too fuzzy right now to try to think it through.

The way he saw it, only two items were blemishing an otherwise charmed life for him. First, this damn injury that kept him drugged at the edge of disaster. And second, his loss of memory regarding the last few years of his life. Other than that, things were coming up roses.

He sighed and went back to sleep.

CHAPTER THREE

JANIS woke to a cooler, darkened room. Someone had come in and turned on a side lamp, but the light it shed was minimal. They had also left a tray with a covered bowl. She rose and went over to take a peek. Chicken soup. She smiled. At least the butler took her seriously.

But the soup had cooled. How long had she been sleeping? She looked around for a clock and didn't find one.

And finally, she looked at Mykal.

Her heart was in her throat again. Just looking at him sent her over the moon. She was in big trouble. How was she going to convince her traitorous heart not to love him? She began to pace the room, hands clenched into fists, thinking furiously, trying to get a handle on her situation.

Obviously, she couldn't stay here. What had she been thinking? The need to make sure Mykal was safe had overwhelmed her good sense. See how he contorted her emotions? She didn't dare stay and let that happen time after time, as it surely would.

She'd come with three objectives and not one of them was in the bag. That was a pretty poor performance. But how could she fight a man who was in such a precarious position? No way. She would just have to leave and hope she could get this close to him again later.

"Or else, send him a sternly worded letter," she muttered to herself ruefully. "Arrgghh."

All right, that was settled. She was leaving. She glanced at him again and winced. He was so darn beautiful. But he made her heart ache with a longing she didn't need right now. She was going. Just exactly where, she didn't know. These last few weeks in the prison camp, all she'd thought about was finding him and confronting him for all the misery she'd been through. It still hurt so badly to know he could have spared her all that if he'd cared enough to lift a finger.

But he hadn't. And now he was the one in trouble. Why should she bother with him?

She shouldn't. It was over.

She was deep in thought but suddenly her senses tingled. Someone was coming into the room behind her. The butler? Another servant? Before she could turn to see who it was, a male voice shot across the room like the flash from a flamethrower.

"Who the hell are you?"

The words hit her from behind but the man's hand was on her neck before the words even registered. She didn't have to think. She reacted on instinct and training, setting her foot and shifting her weight and grabbing the man by the neck. It was all a matter of balance and leverage. She'd done it so often it came naturally, and she slung him over her head, onto the floor. He landed with a grunt and lay very still. She gasped, wondering if she'd killed him.

But then a string of obscenities came pouring out of his mouth and she sighed with relief. Anyone who could swear like that still had a lot of life in him.

"Hey, I'm really sorry," she said, sounding

less than sincere. "But you shouldn't touch a woman without warning like that."

The obscenities didn't stop, and suddenly she realized there was a background sense of chuckling going on. Turning, she found Mykal sitting upright and grinning from ear to ear.

"I see you've met my brother, Kylos," he said, half-laughing. "Wow, as a guard, I'd say you fill the bill. I hope you stay forever."

She flushed. The tiniest hint of praise from him and here she was, blushing. This was crazy and exactly why she couldn't stay.

"Why the hell do you need a guard?" Kylos was grumbling as he clumsily pulled himself to his feet. "A nurse I could understand, but a guard?" He glared at her. "And why did you pick one who shoots first and asks questions later?"

She tried to smile, but it wasn't easy. She'd never even known Mykal had a brother, and this man seemed so unlike him, it was eerie. His face was long and his skin was sallow and he tended to twitch as though he had an itch he was chasing. Where Mykal had been open and welcoming and warm—at least in the past—this man seemed cold and sly and calculating.

And if Mykal had this brother, what else did he have? He'd never told her anything about his family. Looking back now, she realized that their short relationship had been built on some pretty shaky ground. They'd existed in a fantasy bubble of their own. They'd kept their marriage a secret from most of the world, knowing they could lose their jobs if the intelligence service found out. It had seemed daring and exciting at the time. And it had only lasted a few weeks—barely time for them to get to know each other, much less discover anything about their respective families.

Crazy days—but as she remembered them, she couldn't help but smile to herself. If it hadn't ended so badly, just think where they might be now.

"The castle sent her over," Mykal responded, sounding cool and cynical. "She's probably supposed to keep me from killing myself by doing something normal."

She was dying to ask what the castle had to do with this, but if they thought that was who had sent her, any questions on the subject might seem odd. So she decided to fulfill her role instead, raising her hand in warning as he seemed to be leaning forward with a bit too much vigor.

"Careful," she said. "I'm sure the physicians have warned you against any sudden movements."

He sent her an icy look before settling back against the pillows. "I heard their advice. I accept it—for now. They seem to think my life, as I've known it, is fully over with." He looked at her in a way that implied an intimacy he couldn't possibly think they shared, and then his gaze took on a challenging look. "Little do they know. This human hulk will rise again. And that's a promise."

"Not on my watch," she said firmly, chin in the air as she looked back into his frosty eyes. "I haven't lost a patient yet."

"Well, that's encouraging." But his attention was fading and he winced. It was obvious he was still in pain.

Her heart lurched and she had to stop herself from moving toward him. She looked toward the doorway instead. Once she was out again, she wasn't coming back. But then her gaze fell on the bowl of soup.

"You should be hungry by now," she said, reaching for it. "I'll go get this soup heated up for you. You probably want to talk to your brother anyway."

He appeared surprised. "No, not really," he murmured, but she was out the door.

There was no one in the kitchen, but the microwave worked fine and she was back in a flash, more determined than ever to wrap this thing up and take her leave.

"Can you handle this on your own?" she asked Mykal as she set the soup up for him on a bed tray.

He gave her a look but didn't say anything. Taking the bowl from her, he proceeded to drink from it as though it were a large cup. She stood back and tried not to smile. Everything he did, every move he made, caused her to resonate like a tuning fork. The only problem was, each response was paired with a touch of fear at the same time.

His brother was hanging around grimly. He'd turned on the television, seemingly more for background noise than for any programming content. He made a face and gestured at Janis, making it clear he wanted to talk to her alone. She was tempted to go ahead and leave without letting him get his way, but she reluctantly hung back as he drew her aside in order to speak without Mykal overhearing.

"Listen, did they leave any medication for him?" he asked her urgently, leaning close. "I've looked all over and I can't find anything. I was told they would leave something to help keep him quiet."

She nodded, surprised at his intensity. "In the bathroom," she said, pointing it out. "On a shelf in the medicine cabinet, I think."

"Oh. Of course." He looked as though he was starting off in that direction, then he hesitated, grimacing. "I guess that's supposed to be *your* job, right?" He gestured toward Mykal. "Don't you think you ought to give him something? He seems awfully wide-awake to me."

"I think he's allowed a little awake time," she said, feeling slightly annoyed, then realizing she was talking through her hat. For all she knew, Kylos had talked to the doctors himself and knew much more than she did.

But actually, he didn't act like it.

"Oh. Of course," he said, fidgeting. He gave her an arch look. "But we wouldn't want him to hurt himself."

She frowned. "Don't worry. I think he understands the possible consequences."

She moved a little away from him. There was something definitely unpleasant about the man. Funny. Mykal had always been the sort of man who drew people to him. His brother seemed to be just the opposite.

"I think he can probably monitor his own need for the drugs, don't you think?" she added.

He didn't look convinced, but Mykal was holding out his empty bowl and she turned to take it from him and put it down on the top of the dresser.

"That ought to help make you feel a little more alive," she told him.

He nodded, looking at her with a spark of interest in his eyes. "What's your name, guard lady? What shall I call you?"

She took a deep breath. "Janis," she said. And she didn't give her last name.

"Janis?"

He was still frowning, thinking it over as though it might ring a bell. She held her breath.

And then he showed the hint of a smile. "Nice name," he said. His eyes drifted shut again. "Will you still be here when I wake up, Janis?" he asked her softly.

She couldn't answer that. After all, he'd told her to leave earlier. But he didn't seem to remember that.

"I hope you will," he said groggily. "I have some things I want to talk to you about. Later."

"I…I'll try," she said faintly.

He held out his hand and she knew what he wanted. Quickly, she moved closer and took his hand in hers. He smiled and held on tightly, as though he really did need her to anchor his existence. Then his smile faded as he fell quickly into another deep sleep.

She stared at the hand she was holding, then pressed it to her heart and gazed down at him. He looked like a wounded warrior. Her heart filled with love for him. She couldn't help it. No matter what he did, she couldn't seem to shake it. And in truth, she didn't really want to.

Their marriage had been short, barely two months, but oh, so sweet. They had been friends as well as lovers, but the love had been the best. She remembered the night he'd aroused such passion in her, she'd clawed his back with her fingernails. He'd laughed and teased her that he was going to go around without a shirt for the day so everyone could see what a hot woman he had. She'd been mortified, and so apologetic. But he'd just kissed her and before she knew it, they were making love again.

If they could go back to what they had created between them in the short time they were married, before it all fell apart…

But that was dreaming and in her experience, dreams very seldom came true. She'd grown up hard and tough, learning how to defend herself early. Her mother died when she was young and her father was a mobster. He'd been killed in a police raid when she was ten. Her brother, Rolo, had been the only real family she had left, though they had both gone to live with her uncle, Max Gorgonio. Rolo had been the only person who'd ever been close enough to gain her trust, until she'd met Mykal.

Trust. The word tasted bitter on her lips. What good had all that trust done when the rubber hit the road? It melted away like a springtime snowfall and left cold comfort behind.

"Hey, what's the deal?"

She dropped Mykal's hand with a start. She'd forgotten his brother was still here.

"Nothing," she said quickly. "I was just… thinking."

"Oh, yeah?" He gave her a doubtful look. "Well, I've got to go meet…uh…my lawyer. I've got to get going now. Are you going to be here for the night?"

Was she? No. She had to go. Staying wouldn't accomplish anything. She looked back down and sighed. She hated to leave him, but what else could she do?

Kylos twitched, blinking rapidly. "If you are, you can keep an eye on him. But I want to be perfectly clear. I want to make sure he stays quiet, and in order to do that, I think we ought to keep him pretty drugged up."

The way he'd phrased that gave her a

bad feeling and she looked at him, curious. "Drugged up?" she repeated doubtfully.

"Sure. That's what they did in the hospital, didn't they? No one wants to take any chances with that shrapnel thing in his back."

"Oh, I agree. But he doesn't have to be out cold in order to stay quiet, does he?"

He shrugged and looked bored with it all. "Whatever it takes, honey. I'd just as soon you kept him groggy. He's easier to handle that way."

Her mouth dropped. What on earth was this man talking about?

"Hey." He pinched her cheek and grinned at her. "Just play along for now and I'll make sure you get a bonus when this job is over. I just need a couple more days and then…" He twitched nervously and looked as though he was afraid he might have said too much. "What I mean is, I'm really worried about my brother's chances. He's got big things in the works and we have to keep him calm. Get it?"

No, she didn't get it at all, but she nodded. And at the same time, she had a sinking feeling. She wasn't going to leave, was she? Not while this vulture was strutting around asking her to drug Mykal. She couldn't allow that. Someone had to monitor the situation. She sighed. Maybe she would be here for the long haul after all.

Or at least until Mykal's last few years came back to him and he realized that she was his wife—and that he hated her.

She woke up feeling odd. For a moment, she looked around, disoriented. Where in the world was she? And then it flooded back to her and she jerked upright. The bed was empty. Where was Mykal?

She heard water. A shower. The bathroom.

Leaping to her feet, she raced to the bathroom door and flung it open without thinking twice.

"What the heck do you think you're doing?" she demanded into the steamy room.

"Well, hello to you, too." He leaned around the shower curtain, amusement dancing in his eyes. "Care to join me?"

She drew in a sharp breath, realizing this must seem odd to him. At the same time, the sight of his naked body, which was clear at the edge of the shower curtain, did nothing but bring back delicious memories. It was a body she knew only too well—but he didn't know that.

"You're not supposed to do anything without support," she said crisply, making it up as she went along, but pretty sure she had the melody right, if not the exact words. "I'm here to help you. Any sudden moves could kill you!"

He made a face. "Okay, take it easy. I'm not suicidal. But I can make some decisions for myself."

"Not until you clear them with me." She might have gone over the top, but she was genuinely worried. He was being reckless. She had to find a way to make him think things through before he acted.

"Clear them with you?" He looked at her as though she were a slightly annoying insect he could bat away at will. "Sorry. I don't mean to be rude, but you're nothing to me. You're an employee."

Something choked in her throat. He was right, of course. She was nothing to him. Not anymore. She started to turn away, but he seemed to regret his harsh words.

"Wait a minute," he said, calling her back.

She stopped and glanced back at him, hoping he couldn't see how much he'd hurt her. She had no right to be hurt. She was nothing to him. But there was one problem. He was still everything to her. She just needed time to train herself not to care. Slowly, reluctantly, she turned back toward him and waited for his explanation.

"I apologize," he said. "That was uncalled for." He smiled at her, then turned off the water and leaned out. "And anyway, I need you here to hand me a towel."

She made a face, but did as he asked, handing him a nice thick one. He dried himself behind the shower curtain, then wrapped it around his waist and stepped out onto the bath mat, being careful and a bit tentative, but able to manage it on his own. And looking proud of himself for it.

About then she told herself she really ought to be backing out of the bathroom. Ordinarily, with a stranger, she would have been long gone. But being here like this with Mykal felt natural and familiar. And so here she was.

She should have gone. But her body didn't

seem to be obeying orders from the top right now. Every piece of her attention was being soaked up by the sense of the beautiful man standing before her. A few weeks in a coma didn't seem to have sapped away any of that long, lean muscle mass that worked together to form a hard, sleek classic statue of a man, and the memory of what his strong arms had felt like as they tightened around her took her breath away. Her gaze trailed from his wide shoulders down across his gorgeous chest with its fine mat of dark hair.

This was the man she had loved with a crazy passion such a short time ago. Something inside, some insane impulse, told her to throw herself into his arms. That he would remember if she only held him and kissed him like she used to. That all would be forgiven and they would laugh together and make love together and blot out all the bad times as though they had never happened. It was worth a try. Wasn't it?

Everything in her yearned to take the chance.

But then she looked up into his eyes and what she saw there stopped her cold. There was no love. There was no memory. There was only a faintly amused look of surprise. He thought she was being overwhelmed by his manly presence, and he was right. Only, he thought she was an employee who could be flirted with, to a point, but needed to be kept at arm's length. And she wasn't.

Taking a deep breath, she tried to get her bearings and get back to the job at hand.

"Uh…" She swallowed hard and lifted her chin, blinking in the light. "Listen, playing Russian roulette is not just a fun option. It's risking your life. And I'm supposed to make sure you don't do that."

His frown was stubborn. "But that's just it. It's *my* life. It belongs to me. Not you. Not the doctors. Not the wise guys at the castle. Just me."

He was right, but it made her want to cry. She couldn't explain to him why she felt she had a stake in this situation. She couldn't tell him much.

He hitched up the towel and gave her a look of pure skepticism. She drew in her breath, startled by his distrust. Still, he was so beautiful, she was tempted to start letting her gaze travel over him again, a simple, guilty pleasure. But his look suddenly hardened, as though he'd remembered she was an interloper and wasn't sure why she was still hanging around.

"So let's get this straight," he was saying. "I'll do things at my own pace. You can give advice. But you're not going to set any agendas. I'll do that." He gave her a challenging look. "No rules."

She nodded reluctantly. "Okay." She drew in a deep breath. "But…"

"Uh-uh." He shook his head. "This is my game. I'll play it my way. If you can't handle that, it's time for you to go."

CHAPTER FOUR

JANIS'S pivot wasn't graceful but at least she didn't fall on her face, shaky as she was. He couldn't have been clearer. He wanted her gone. She headed back into the room and reached for her satchel. This time she really would go. If he wanted to risk ruining his life, she wasn't going to try to stop him.

She stopped and looked around the room, making sure she wasn't leaving anything. She was angry and feeling wounded. She'd only been trying to help. She'd had enough.

Where would she go? She wasn't sure. It was getting pretty late. This was a nice neighborhood. Maybe there was a hotel nearby. Maybe. If not, she would wander around until she got her bearings. She only hoped she wouldn't have to end up sleeping under a bridge in the cold.

One last glance back over her shoulder and she was stepping out the door. And that was the moment she heard his gasp of pain.

She was back in the room in a flash. He was leaning against the doorjamb, his eyes closed.

"Oh, no, oh, no," she whispered like a prayer as she rushed to help him. He'd managed to put on pajama bottoms, but his chest was still bare. She quickly slipped under his shoulder and became a crutch for him.

"What happened?" she asked.

His mouth twisted into something resembling a sort of grin, but he shook his head. "I'm just too damn weak to support myself once the pain starts shooting through me," he muttered, sounding resentful.

"Lean on me," she told him firmly. "Come on. I'll get you back into bed."

He felt like heaven, even this way—all hard muscle and slick skin. She turned her face toward him and took in his familiar smell and then wished she hadn't. Emotion came surging up her throat. She'd missed him so.

She hardened her heart and forced herself to hold him steady as they made their way across the floor. And then she had him at the edge of the bed and he groaned as he slid down onto the covers.

For just a moment, she caught a glimpse of his back, at the horrible red scarring, and her heart lurched. Horror shivered through her and then she steadied herself and thought of basics instead of pain.

Where was his brace? He should be in it. And surely he'd had bandages on the wounds when he'd been brought in here. He must have taken them off when he went into the shower. Should he have done that? She highly doubted it. But there wasn't much she could do about it right now. He'd been very clear. This was his game. Carefully, she pulled the sheets from under him and then pulled them over and tucked him in, looking down at him anxiously.

He was looking up at her. He didn't smile, but there was something going on behind his crystal gaze.

"Okay," he said roughly. "Just let me rest a minute."

She nodded, thankful he seemed to be tired but largely okay. She resisted the impulse to tell him to wiggle his toes and prove nothing had touched his spinal cord at this point. Making a quick trip back into the bathroom, she saw where he'd thrown away the old bandaging. She opened the cabinet and grabbed a round of tape and a package of fresh gauze pads, snagged the brace and took it all back out into the bedroom.

His eyes were open and he looked alert, but he shook his head when he saw what she had.

"I want to let air get to it," he told her.

She hesitated, not sure that was a good idea, but she couldn't argue with him, could she? With a sigh, she put her supplies down and sank onto the couch.

"You always have to do it your way, don't you?" she grumbled.

He was feeling better by the minute and he managed a lopsided smile. "Is it that obvious?" he asked. "I'd almost think you knew me well."

That was putting it mildly. It was very strange to realize that he didn't remember anything about the last two years, and especially that he didn't have any of the past they'd shared in his system. They hadn't been together long, but it had certainly changed her life. To think any changes he'd gone through were lost, or reversed, or whatever had happened to them, was unsettling to say the least. She didn't like it. It just might be that when he remembered, he would hate her again. But that would be better than not remembering and being untouched by all they had gone through together.

The way he was watching her, his head back, his eyes half-closed, she wasn't sure what he was thinking. The seconds stretched out longer and longer. He didn't speak, but he kept looking at her. She bit her lip, nervous but ready to deal with whatever he was getting ready to throw at her. Somehow she knew it was coming.

But when he finally spoke, his question was awkward for her, but rather ordinary in its way.

"Are you married?" he asked at last.

Her heart lurched, but she managed to hide it. "Yes," she said quickly. "Yes, I am. But we're pretty much separated right now."

"I see." He nodded slowly. "The war."

"Yes. The war." She almost laughed aloud. "Blame it on the war." Why not? The war had been the supposed reason behind everything in their relationship so far.

He frowned. "I was in the war. So they tell me. I don't remember." He twitched as though he wasn't really comfortable. "They say I did some good things, but I guess I'll never know for sure."

"Well, of course," she said with a smile that quickly turned bittersweet.

Something told her that he knew, without having to be told, that he'd been brave and honorable. It was the essence of who he was. And it was also why they were so badly matched. The ache in the bottom of her heart seemed to throb more painfully than ever. You could change your mind, you could change your behavior, but you couldn't change your bloodline.

"When do you go home?" he asked.

"I was just leaving when you collapsed," she said defensively. "I'll go. Don't worry."

He frowned at her, seeming furious all of a sudden. "Why would you go?" he demanded. "Isn't it your job to stay here with me?"

"Not when you kick me out like you did."

"Kick you out?" He obviously thought she was making things up. "I would never kick you out. I need you. Has anyone made up a room for you?"

"No." She looked at him, exasperated and confused. "Actually, I haven't told anyone I need one yet. I thought…"

He moved impatiently. "Get Boswell in here. He'll make sure you have good accommodations. I'm surprised he didn't take it upon himself to do it already."

She stared at him blankly. "Boswell?"

"Our butler."

She wrinkled her nose. "I thought his name was Griswold."

"Oh." He grimaced as though he'd just remembered something best left to the shadows. "That's right. Kylos replaced the entire staff for some ungodly reason." He frowned fiercely at her. "Do you know why he did that?"

"Uh…no."

"Neither do I." He sighed, looking restless. "Poor old Boswell. I wonder what's happened to him? He was here from the time I was a toddler. Practically part of the family."

"Well, now you've got Griswold. But he went home at nine o'clock."

He stared at her, nonplussed. "Went home! What the hell's a butler doing going home? Doesn't he live here, in the house?"

She threw up her hands and laughed at him. "I don't know. He's your butler."

The situation seemed to bother him. "Boswell wouldn't have left his post," he muttered to himself.

She nodded, sure that was true. But then, she'd never had a butler. The thought made her want to giggle. She only hoped it wasn't plain old hysteria threatening.

Because this entire situation was strangely weird and getting weirder. She certainly felt tugged in two directions. She had a deep underlying feeling she ought to have kept going once she was on her way out a few minutes before. And at the same time, she wanted to stay. She wanted to make sure he was okay. Not only was she worried about his condition, but there was also something about his brother that didn't sit well with her.

Or was she rationalizing again?

"Hey," she said as she noticed he was sitting up and beginning to swing his legs over the side of the bed. "What are you doing now?"

He stopped, eyeing her with a certain cool moodiness. "I'm doing whatever I feel like doing. And right now, I've got a yen to see my old house."

"You mean, this one?"

He nodded. "If I've got another, I don't remember it." He gazed at her levelly. "I'm counting on you to be my crutches. To catch me when I fall. Okay?"

She was tempted to argue with him but she knew it would do no good. "Sure," she said wryly. "I'm adjustable. That's why they pay me the big bucks."

"Don't go expecting diamonds and pearls from me," he said, teasing. His grin was lop-sided. "But play your cards right and if this royal thing comes through, I might be able to buy you an iced latte one of these days."

"I'm excited," she said, a trace of sarcasm showing. But she was smiling as she rose to help him up. He leaned on her lightly with one hand on her shoulder and they walked slowly out onto the beautifully finished maple floors on into the foyer with its marble inlays. She took the time to look around and appreciate how much care someone had taken in making this home a beautiful showplace. The fact that the décor was about fifty years out-of-date didn't matter. The warmth and character of the home shone through.

He took her through the study and into the library, where the walls were filled with floor-to-ceiling, glass-enclosed bookcases full of books. They strolled through the kitchen and she realized it had only been the butler's pantry she'd visited before. The central kitchen was huge with large ovens of all kinds and a refrigerator that took up one wall.

"We used to have huge parties," he told her. "And people staying for the weekend. There was always something going on. But that was before…" His voice seemed to trail off.

"Before?" she asked, but he ignored her and went on, pointing out the herb garden from the kitchen window.

"Let's go upstairs," he said. "You can see

almost the whole estate laid out in front of you from my old room."

She thought she'd caught signs already that he was flagging a bit. "Mykal, do you think you should?"

"Sure I should." He grinned at her. "We'll take the elevator."

"You have an elevator in your house?"

"Sure. My father got very weak after...after some financial reverses and this house has three levels."

The elevator swayed a bit, but it got them there.

"Here's my bedroom," he said, leading her in and pointing out the bay window. "I used to sit on this window seat and stare out for hours."

She could see why. Night had fallen but the place was littered with solar lamps that flickered from the trees and from the side of walkways. It seemed to be an enchanted garden. But she was more interested in looking at the artifacts of his boyhood that filled the shelves, books and trains and bats and soccer balls.

"Your parents left a lot of your things here,

almost on display. You know what that means, don't you?" She looked at him teasingly.

He shrugged. "That they were too lazy to throw it all out?"

"No. That they loved you so much they wanted to hang on to everything that reminded them of you."

He smiled as though what she'd said had touched him, just a little. "Yeah. My mom likes me."

She looked at him and thought, *Who wouldn't?* He was such a charmer. Her eyes met his and she realized he was still thinking about what she'd said. Was he missing his parents? How sad. Funny that he'd never told her about them at all.

"How could they have left this beautiful house?" she asked him.

"You should have seen it when I was a kid. The estate was twice this big and the condition was ten times better. Financial reverses did my father in about fifteen years ago."

That made her curious. "Where did they go?" she asked. "To the continent?"

"No." He flashed her a quick look. "Believe it or not, they went to Florida and bought a condominium and have been quite happy ever since. I don't think they'll ever come back." His eyebrows knit together and he looked at her as though he found that hard to believe.

She nodded, suppressing the trace of a grin. "Some people like sunshine on the water."

"As opposed to fog and rain clouds?" His smile was quick and humorless as he described the usual weather in Ambria to a T. "I suppose."

They were standing very close and he turned, putting his hand on her shoulder for a moment, as though to balance himself. Then his face changed and he moved closer, leaning in, spreading his fingers over the small of her back.

"You did say you were married, right?" he asked, his voice low and musical.

"Yes." She looked away. "Technically, I'm married."

He touched her chin with his finger. "No hope of getting back together?"

She met his crystal gaze and shook her head. "No."

He raised an eyebrow. "You're sure?"

"Positive."

"Good." He pushed her hair back behind her ear. "Because I want to kiss your neck."

"What?" She reacted, but she didn't really pull away. How could she when every nerve in her body was reacting as though violins were playing?

"Don't move, now," he said in a soft, half-teasing voice. "I'm a sick man, you know. I must be humored."

"That's outrageous." But she was laughing low in her throat. "And it's cheating, too."

"I'll have to plead guilty to that." His breath was warm on her skin. "But something about you makes me crazy. I can't stay away."

His face was nuzzling her neck by now, and then she felt his tongue, sending shivers all through her system.

"Mykal," she said, and her voice almost sounded like a whimper. She turned her face and he brushed his cheek against hers. And then he'd pulled back, as though nothing had ever happened.

The look in his eyes as he cupped her cheek with the palm of his hand was heavy with a sensual vibe that made her blood feel like maple syrup. "You're pregnant, aren't you?" he said simply.

Shock slashed through her like a lightning bolt and her eyes went very wide. How could he tell? No one knew. She hadn't told a soul and she was still so thin from the prison camp ordeal.

"I...uh...no..." she stammered.

"Don't worry. I can keep a secret." His wide mouth twisted in a half smile. "But I thought I could tell when you were helping me to the bed. I could sense it." He looked at her with a sense of regret. "I hope it's true. You should be very happy."

She glanced away, but her throat was choked and there was no way she could force out any words. How on earth could he tell? She'd been sure it would be weeks before anyone would see it. Did he remember...? But no, there was nothing to remember. He'd never known. She hadn't even known until she was in the prison camp.

Was it because he was the father? Did he have some special, magical sense of his own child? It seemed impossible. And yet...

He led her to a guest room and showed her

the view along the other side, one that was partly lit with electric lights. She followed him willingly. It was almost as though he'd hypnotized her now.

"Take a look out here. There's the duck pond. Too bad it doesn't look like anyone's maintained it for a long time."

She loved the quaint setting. "What's that burned-out house behind it?"

He didn't answer for a moment and she realized that he was too emotional to speak at first. Then he cleared his throat and said, "That was my mother's Victorian tea house. She loved having her friends over for high tea. They would sit on the little porch and watch the ducks and eat their watercress sandwiches and sip their Darjeeling. Nothing made her happier."

She hesitated to ask when he was so affected by it, but her curiosity was running wild. "What happened to it?"

He took a deep breath. "Long story. Bottom line, enemies of my father burned it down."

How awful. "What? Why would anyone do such a thing?"

"There are bad people in this world, Janis."

He touched her cheek again, but playfully this time. "Stay away from them if you can."

"I try to. Were your parents hurt?"

He looked at her in surprise, then smiled. "This happened years ago. My father left it that way as a reminder."

"I see." Though she didn't, not really.

He stood brooding over the view for a few more minutes, and she waited, not wanting to break into his reverie.

"Okay, here's what happened," he said at last, as though he just couldn't hold it in any longer. He reached out to use her shoulder, leaning on her as though his legs were getting tired. "Well, my father made some bad decisions. Kylos got into some trouble. He was always getting into trouble, but this time it was really bad. My father needed money fast, but times were tight, and he couldn't find anyone who could lend him that much. So in the end, he had to turn to the mob."

At the sound of that three-letter word, disbelief filled her. This couldn't be happening. She'd never heard a whisper of it. Her heart turned to stone and something deep inside her began to pray. *Please, please, please, don't let it be the Gorgonios.*

"It was a lot of money and he couldn't pay it back. He went into hiding for a long time. My poor, tiny little mother had to fend for herself." Anger began to boil up in him. "The police could keep the mob from hurting her, but they couldn't keep them from ruining her financially. She was just barely able to hold on to the house. But in the meantime, they did burn down my mother's tea house, just to make sure we knew they were serious."

She murmured something, hoping it sounded sympathetic, but there was a loud buzzing in her ears. Was she going to faint?

"Everyone knows what happens when you don't pay off your loan in time to a member of the mob. They ruin your life or they break your legs." His laugh was humorless. "My father was lucky. He still has his legs. He finally pulled together the resources from some old friends and came back, paid off the loan and eventually all was well. But it took him years to get back into shape as far as money went and it broke their health in the meantime. And so they finally gave up and went overseas to live."

"Oh." It sounded to her as if she were drowning, but he didn't seem to notice. He was caught up in his story.

He looked at her and suddenly his hand slipped around her shoulders, pulling her in close. "I guess you know that in Ambria, the mob means the Gorgonios. Luckily, I recently heard that most of the family is in prison. Especially Max Gorgonio, the lousy bastard. I say don't rest until you get them all behind bars."

She could hardly breathe. Would he still want her if he knew she was one of them? She flailed about fruitlessly, trying to find a way to change the subject. Turning toward him, she was horrified and confused, and he took her emotion to be something very different. Softly, slowly, he kissed her lips, and she found herself curling in against his warm body, hungering for more, yearning for the strength and protection he could provide.

"Oh, Mykal," she whispered so softly he couldn't hear. "If you only knew..."

"Sorry," he murmured as he pulled back.

"There's something about you that just calls to me."

She searched his eyes. There was still no depth in his feeling for her. Still no memories. But his warm and wonderful kiss was a start.

She winced, remembering his family's encounter with her notorious uncle. How she wished she could blot that out forever. The most hated crime family in Ambria, and it had to be hers.

It was tragic, really. The more she tried to distance herself from her background, the more it seemed to crop up all around her. She wasn't a crook and she hated being associated with some really terrible people, people she was tied to by blood. But not by choice. Never that.

Suddenly she noticed that Mykal was getting more tired than she'd realized.

"I've got to sit down for a few minutes," he told her, grimacing as he moved his leg. "Just give me a minute here."

She helped him sit on the bed, then sat beside him. He took her hand in his and laced fingers.

"Kylos says he's contacted our parents about my accident and they may be coming soon," he told her, trying to take deep, cleansing breaths. "I told him to let them know I'd rather they stay put. They're a little old to go rampaging around the world." He shrugged. "And it's probably just as well they aren't here, considering what's happening."

She looked up, wary. "Do you mean…?"

He nodded. "This whole royal thing. I suppose you've heard about it. Everyone seems to know." But he was frowning, searching her face.

She hesitated, wondering if she should pretend to know what the heck he was referring to. But she didn't have a clue. Pretending would only give her more to trip over.

"I don't have any idea what you're talking about," she admitted at last.

He looked incredulous. "You really don't know?"

She shook her head. In for a penny, in for a pound. "I've been out of town on a field assignment," she said carefully, trying not to put it in terms he would recognize from their undercover work. "I haven't had time to pick up a paper or listen to the news for weeks." She gave him a quick smile. "I'm as innocent as a newborn child. So tell me. Why are you so popular at the castle these days?"

"Interesting." He raised an eyebrow and gave her a teasing smile. "I'm the one with amnesia, but I have to fill you in on what's happening. You're in worse shape than I am."

"Oh, just tell me," she said impatiently.

He shrugged. "It's simple, really." He gave her a teasing smile. "Do I look like a royal prince to you?"

She frowned. That was something she'd never thought of. "No."

"Me neither. But people at the castle seem to think I do."

"Ignore them," she said. It was her instant reaction.

He laughed. "It's tempting to do that. But someone at the castle has gotten it into their head that I'm one of the long-lost princes we always used to hear legends about. You know, the ones who disappeared the night the castle burned, during the rebellion that brought the Granvillis into power."

She stared at him, stunned. "But…wait…"

He gave a short laugh. "Yes, that's exactly what I said when they first told me."

She shook her head. This was incredible. "That would mean…"

"That I was adopted by the parents who raised me." He shrugged. "Yes, but I've known that for years."

Her eyes widened. "So it is possible."

"Yes. Possible. Not necessarily probable."

Her head was spinning. Mykal, royal? That was just so crazy on so many levels. "And so…?"

"Blood samples have been taken. Physicians have been poring over my painfully crumpled body. Psychologists have been analyzing my poor puzzled brain." His tone was world-weary and cynical. "Analysts have tried to trip me up and prove I'm lying."

"About what?"

He shrugged. "Anything, mostly about when I was eight years old. What I called my mother. Where I hid when I was afraid my father was mad at me. The name of my first toy horse."

She sat back, almost dazed. "Wow."

He nodded. "Believe me, it's been no bed

of roses. This royalty gig is not for the faint of heart. They put you through the wringer."

She stared at him. Royal. Could it really be true? An ache started deep in her heart. She knew what this was—a death knell for her marriage. Sure, she'd told herself it was all over many times in the last few weeks, but there had always been a small, pitiful hope in the furthest reaches of her soul. Now that hope was dying.

Royalty. That was a bridge too far for her to go. He had no idea, had never had a clue, just how far from royalty her family was. Neither one of them had thought twice about what sort of families they came from. They hadn't given a thought to where they planned to go in life. There was a war on and they both had dangerous jobs. Love and passion were all they cared about. Nothing else mattered. They had to be together every possible moment, and when they weren't, all their energy went into keeping their relationship a secret from their respective commanding officers. Any hint of a marriage would have had them both out on their ears.

Under normal circumstances they would

have begun to ask each other questions in time. But they never got the chance. It was all over much too soon. When he'd walked in to their bedroom and found her going through his hidden papers…

She drew in a shuddering breath, pushing that awful memory away, and tried to keep calm. "And what are the results?"

He shook his head, wondering why she seemed so emotional about something that was only happening to him. He appreciated the concern, but it seemed a bit extreme. "Tests are ongoing."

A lost Ambrian prince. Incredible. That changed everything.

CHAPTER FIVE

"WHY does this house seem so empty?"

Janis and Mykal were downstairs again, walking arm-in-arm through the kitchen into the foyer.

"Because the people have gone," Mykal answered her. "All we've got left are the ghosts of lives gone by."

As if on cue, the sound of provocative feminine laughter came at them from down the hallway and they both came to a shocked standstill.

"Ghosts?" she whispered, glancing at him sideways.

He frowned. "I'm putting my money on flesh and blood in this case," he muttered, starting for where the sound came from.

The evidence of someone having a good time seemed to be coming from the library.

The feminine simpering had been joined by a deeper male voice, seemingly egging her on. As they reached the door, Mykal held out his arm.

"Stand back. You might not want to see this," he warned.

She half laughed. "But you do?"

"It's my duty," he said with a wink. The door came open and the giggling came to an abrupt halt. All Janis could see over his shoulder was a flash of frilly skirt and Mykal's brother's angry face as he jumped up off the couch.

"Okay, Kylos," Mykal said in his best authoritative voice. "You want to explain this?"

"What the hell, Mykal? You could knock on the door, you know."

"And you could lock it if you plan some really heavy lovemaking here."

"I...I...no, I..."

"Who is this lovely young lady?"

She was giggling again and now Janis could see her plainly. A little too blond and a little too old for Kylos, she was still pretty, but didn't look too bright.

"This is our cook," Kylos said angrily. "I

hired her yesterday. I was just conferring with her. I have to do that, you know."

Mykal was obviously holding back a hoot of laughter. "I suppose you do. I'd suggest she could probably understand your instruction better if you left her clothes on, though."

The "cook" was giggling again. Mykal shook his head and gave up. "I hope she knows how to make a good lasagna," he noted as he turned away. Janis hid her smile and followed him to the bedroom he was using. There were no more festive sounds coming from the library.

"I think you ruined their party spirit," she said.

"I hope so," he replied. Turning, he captured her for a moment, looking deep into her eyes. "Just wait. When I'm healthy, I'll be chasing you around the place."

"In your dreams." But she was smiling. Despite everything, she loved him more than life itself.

She helped him get back into bed and she could see by the strain in his face that he'd probably overdone it. She wished he would listen and take it easy. She could see he was in pain again. If only he would listen.

Mykal tried to avoid wincing as his back cramped up. This was what the pain medication was for, but when he took it, he paid too high a price. He was going to try to tough it out. He needed his head clear so that he could think about what was about to happen to him. He wasn't sure, at this stage, that he liked it.

He'd always considered himself a free spirit. Some had even called him untameable at one point in his life. And now he had a chance to be one of the royals? One of those people who drank tea with their pinkies sticking out? One of those miserable bastards who stood around in dress uniforms at boring luncheons? One of those sad sacks who followed daily schedules drawn up for them by weaselly assistants who insisted on rules being followed? That wasn't the life for him. He would smother in that thick pea-soup sort of atmosphere. If that was what it was all about, better that he turn it down right away and save everybody a lot of time.

But he wasn't sure yet. He needed some

time, some space. He needed to think. Looking at Janis, he knew he needed something else, too, but as far as he could tell, he didn't have a woman of his own. Once the pain faded a bit, maybe he could find one—maybe one who looked as good as this one sitting across from him. He grimaced, fighting back the thought. Messing around with employees was never a good idea.

Still, he enjoyed her sinuous movements and the way the two ribbons of her silvery-blond hair linked around her collarbone. Surely she had a man in her life. Some guy was lucky to have her.

That was what he needed, someone just like Janis. A woman who captivated the imagination as well as the libido. Someone with a soft, provocative touch and a sensual smolder. He had vague stirrings just thinking about it. He looked into her eyes.

"Ready for some medication?" she asked hopefully.

He smiled. "Why would I need medication when I have you?"

"Oh, brother." She loved that he flirted with her, but she hated it, too—and that was

a reaction she didn't even want to begin analyzing.

She wished she could help him. If he knew
she was his wife, would he let her do more?
If she told him who she really was, could he
stay calm? Should she go ahead and do it?
That was the question that was torturing her.

He wouldn't remember what had happened
anyway. But if he knew they were married,
that they had once been in love, then he might
be able to accept her in the role of his wife
and she could make these decisions for him,
give him better support. But until she assumed that place in his life, how could she
dare to even try?

She examined his bandages and brace and
then looked back at him. He seemed so unpro-
tected. And he was moving too much. Maybe
he should take the medication. It had been a
long time since the medics had given him that
last dose. Yes. She made up her mind. She'd
hesitated, mostly because of his brother being
so strangely insistent. But now she knew it
was necessary.

"I think it's time you took something," she
said, trying to sound brisk and professional,

rising from the couch. "It's been over four hours. I'll just go into the bathroom and…"

"No." He said it with a finality that quite put an end to the matter. "I'm not going to take any more of that stuff. I want to clear my head and begin to live again."

She drew her breath in, tottering between decisions. "But, if it was prescribed for you… It keeps you still and that is what we want."

"If the pain gets too bad, I'll let you know. I'm not a masochist. But for the first time in weeks my mind is clearing and I can think things through again. I no longer feel as though demons were flying around in my head."

She sighed. "Sober is always better." She admitted.

"Anything that's an antibiotic or something I need directly in order to heal, I will gladly take. Medication just to keep me drowsy, or even just to deal with pain, I'd rather hold off on that until I really need it. I've been under heavy sedation too much lately. I don't want to go there again."

He was firm on this. She could tell he

wasn't going to budge an inch. Sighing, she sat down again.

"Then please, please just stay quiet," she told him earnestly. "At least until you see the doctor tomorrow."

He nodded, but he wasn't all that convincing. She was having a hard time herself. The way they had been on their little expedition around the house had brought up memories of how they'd been when they were in love. And then to think that her family had caused his family such pain—that alone should make a relationship between the two of them a no-go at this point. It would never, never work again.

"Are you hungry?" she asked, needing to leave the room and looking for an excuse.

"A little."

"You should eat something." She frowned, thinking it was important even as a hedge against the very drugs he wanted to avoid. If Kylos came back and talked him into taking more medication, it would help if he had some food in his stomach. "Do you want me to warm up some more of that chicken soup?"

He shook his head, making a face.

"I know." She brightened as she remembered. "I'll go make you a cheese omelet. Your favorite."

He looked at her in surprise. "How did you know that was my favorite?"

She stopped, stunned that she'd made a mistake like that. For just a moment, she couldn't think of a thing to say and she stared at him, deer in the headlights.

"I…I didn't," she finally improvised. "But I assume eggs and cheese are bound to be in the refrigerator, even if nothing else is. So I thought I'd go with that."

He was still frowning at her. She gave him a bright smile and left the room, leaning against the wall in the hallway once she was clear and trying to catch her breath. That had been a clumsy move. She was going to have to do better than that if she was going to survive this little adventure.

But wait. Just how long did she plan to let this masquerade go? She knew she couldn't leave until someone else came to watch over him, but once that happened, was she going to leave at last? Shaking her head, she headed to the kitchen. She had no answer for her own questions.

She walked into the kitchen and looked around, hoping she wasn't going to run into the so-called cook. She was lucky. There was no sign of anyone. But she was cooking the omelet when Kylos came in through the outer door. He immediately threw out his hands like a gunfighter showing he wasn't near his guns.

"Hey, babe, I'm not going to scare you this time. So no fair trying to take me down, okay?"

"No problem," she said as she flipped the perfectly cooked omelet onto a porcelain plate. "As long as you come in peace, I'll be peaceful."

"I just got back from taking the cook home." He looked at the food appreciatively and sniffed the air. "Hey, can you make me one of those?"

She gave him a look. "Do you have shrapnel wounds all over your back?" she asked.

He looked pained. "You know the answer to that."

"Then you know my answer as well." But she said it loud and clear, just to be sure. "No."

He took it calmly and sighed as she walked past with the plate in her hand. "Pity," he muttered. "Hey, we need to talk."

But she just kept going. Now that Mykal had told her about being adopted, she could see why the two of them were so different. Brothers in nurture, not in nature. But was Mykal really royal? Yikes.

"Your brother is back," she told Mykal as she pushed open the door and made her way into the room. "Do you trust him?"

His eyes widened in surprise. "Kylos? Why, did he make a pass at you?"

"I can handle passes from men like Kylos," she said scornfully as she set up his eating situation. "What I want to know is, do you have reason to suspect him of ulterior motives?"

He shook his head, not sure what she was getting at. "For what?"

She shrugged. "I don't know. He just seems a little devious."

"Devious." He grinned and picked up a fork. "Kylos always has ulterior motives. And he's very often devious. So you're right on both counts. Watch your step around him."

And he began to eat the omelet. Very quickly, his time was taken up by sounds of epicurean pleasure.

She watched him for a moment, glad he seemed to enjoy the food. But she was worried about Kylos. She didn't trust him. Still, she really didn't have any evidence of anything substantive, did she? If she tried to tell him her intelligence work training had developed antennae that had always proven uncannily accurate, he would begin asking questions she didn't want to answer.

"So do you have anything you can pin on him right now?" Mykal asked her.

"No," she said at last. "If feelings don't count, I've got nothing."

"Feelings, huh?" He pushed away his half-eaten meal and hummed a few bars of a song, looking off into the distance as though trying to remember something.

She felt herself flushing. She remembered it all only too well. She remembered what a great tenor voice he had and how he loved to sing. He'd sung love songs to her. He'd sung comic songs to make her laugh. All at once, she was dying to hear that beautiful voice again, hear it in full voice. She turned her face away so he wouldn't see that her eyes were misting over.

He began to drift off to sleep. This time he didn't seem to need her hand to hold. She assumed that meant whatever he was taking that made him artificially drowsy had mostly worn off.

She'd pulled a comforter out of the closet and she used it now, curling up on the little couch again after turning down the lights. Just as she was falling asleep, she heard a sound and looked up quickly, just catching a glimpse of Kylos in the doorway before he disappeared. That startled her, but she was too tired to worry about it.

"Tomorrow," she promised herself. "Tomorrow I'll have it out with him." And her eyes closed two seconds later.

Mykal was on his own, walking in the garden. He felt as if he'd escaped from some sort of tender trap, a silken-threads sort of imprisonment, where they tortured you with kindness. He'd slipped out at dawn without waking Janis, found his father's old walking stick in the hall closet and now he was free.

Not that he was going anywhere. In fact, now that the adrenaline of sneaking out had died down, he was beginning to feel the pain again. Also the weakness. Not to mention the cold wind. He wouldn't be able to go much farther. He stopped beside what had once been his favorite pond. It was empty now and he lowered himself carefully to sit on the bench that sat close by. He felt sad to see the bare concrete form without water, and without the colorful koi that had splashed about here when he'd been younger. He frowned, wondering why Kylos was letting the place go this way. He would have to speak to him about it.

But right now, he didn't want to dwell on that. He'd come out here to try and get his head straight. He had to think and decide what he wanted to do with his life, before others made that decision for him. The way things were going, it looked like he just might be the lost prince. Wow. Wonderful. What was that going to do for him? He took a deep breath and frowned. That and a half-crown coin might get him a pint at the local pub.

Hey. He smiled wryly to himself. Maybe it actually would. Maybe people did give princes free food and drink just for showing up at their place. If so, it might actually be worth something.

But he had to get serious and be practical. Did he really want to become a prince and go to live in the castle with the rest of the royal family? Offhand, he didn't think he was suited for the job. It seemed superfluous. He had half a mind to tell them to take their royal crown and… Well, if he did turn it down, he probably wouldn't be quite that rude about it. But he was tempted just to say no.

And yet, he didn't want to be too impulsive. What if there were more to it? What if he could step in and find an important job to do? What if being royal could really put him into a position where he could make a difference?

Probably a pipe dream. Still, this was all sort of interesting, being tapped as a possible lost prince and all. It wasn't quite as good as being a war hero, of course, but it was something. He'd been told he'd done some pretty good things in the war, and he hoped that was true. But what good did it do if you couldn't remember it?

When you got right down to it, it all seemed so pointless. He'd never wanted to be a prince. Most of his childhood had been spent wanting desperately to be a football star. As that dream died, others took its place. He wanted to be a fireman. Then an astronaut. And finally he'd settled on architecture. He'd had a thriving business, but the war had loomed and he remembered thinking being a spy would be great fun. They told him that was exactly what he'd become, though he didn't remember it at all.

But a prince? No, that had never been on his horizon and he wasn't really sure what royalty did beside stand around and look important. Was it really a full-time job? Or were you allowed to follow other pursuits on the side? Someone would have to explain all these little details to him at some point, and then he would make the final determination whether he would submit to the royal rigmarole or not.

Still, it wasn't really filling his mind with eager thoughts. In some ways, it seemed almost irrelevant. His own two lost years were more of an obsession. That was what he couldn't stop thinking about. Where had he been? What had he done? Whom had he offended? Whom had he made love to?

Two years. A lot could happen in that amount of time. He could remember how excited he'd been to begin his military career. He'd prepared himself in every way he could think of. He'd worked out and read books and agonized over his own belief system. He'd filled out the paperwork.

And then—nothing. It was as though he'd walked through a door into another world and stayed there for two years. Now he was back and he wanted to retrieve what he'd lost.

Loss. The word resonated with him. Yes, that was what he was feeling, why he was so restless and dissatisfied. He felt loss— and not just of time and experience. He felt a deep, dark, aching loss in his soul. He needed someone. Something was missing.

He started to stand and the pain hit him

like a knife in the back. Gasping, he fell back down onto the bench. For the moment, pain was all there was.

Janis was muttering to herself as she hurried through the house toward the backyard. She'd overslept and then she'd had to deal with a little bit of morning sickness, something she hadn't had until recently. Now she didn't know where Mykal was and she was furious with herself.

"If I'm going to make a fool of myself hanging around here, I might at least do a good job of keeping tabs on the man," she muttered aloud. "What is the point if I'm not even vigilant?"

She'd woken up, pulled together her clothes and dashed through the house finding absolutely nobody. He had to be outside. She was out the door and into a garden that must have been beautiful once, but had gone a bit too much to seed lately. And then she saw Kylos and Griswold on either side of Mykal, bringing him back to the house.

She gasped. He looked terrible, drawn and pale. The two men were holding all his weight and practically carrying him along. Her heart was in her throat as she ran out to meet them.

"What happened?" she cried.

Kylos gave her a murderous look. "I guess his pain medication wore off and he decided to go gallivanting around," he said coldly. "Too bad you can't be bothered to make sure he's medicated."

"No," Mykal murmured, shaking his head. "I don't want any pain medication."

"What you want and what you need are two different things," Kylos told him sternly.

The house phone began to ring, adding to the sense of frenzy.

"Oh," Janis said, reluctant to leave them but knowing there was no one else to answer the phone in the house. These three were definitely occupied. "Shall I...?"

"If you please, miss," Griswold said, staggering under Mykal's weight. "I'm afraid I'm tied up at the moment."

"If you wouldn't mind," Kylos added through clenched teeth, his eyes shooting daggers.

"Of course." She threw a pained glance at Mykal and a glare back at Kylos and ran into the house and then headed for the study, picking it up in the nick of time.

"Hello," she said breathlessly, looking back to see where they were taking Mykal. "This is the Marten residence."

"This is Queen Pellea," the musical voice on the other end announced in a friendly manner. "I'd like to speak to Mykal, please."

"Oh." Janis stood as though struck dumb. It was the queen. She'd never spoken to a queen before. "Oh, my goodness."

"Is he available?" Her voice rose as she began to intuit that something might be amiss. "What's wrong? Has something happened to him? Please, fill me in right away."

Janis could hear the emotional connection in her voice and for some reason, it touched her heart and caused all her own emotions to come pouring out. Suddenly, she found herself talking to the queen as though she'd known her all her life.

"Oh, Your Royal Highness," she said, not sure if she had the right address but too upset to care. Looking around again, she could see that the men were taking him back into the bedroom. She needed to get to him. She needed to help.

"I've been trying to keep him quiet," she said quickly, "but you can't believe how hard it is. I just woke up to find he's been out running around in the yard and of course now he's collapsed and...and..."

"Okay," Pellea said briskly. "We're moving up the timetable. I'm sending someone over as soon as possible with an ambulance. I want him here at the castle where we can keep an eye on him."

"Oh." She swallowed. She supposed that was probably for the best, but it seemed sudden.

"What is your name, dear?"

She drew in her breath sharply. She had so many names to sift through before deciding what name to give. There was her natural name, Janis Gorgonio, a name that would send up red flags anywhere it was mentioned. Then there was Marten, her married name. And Davos, her mother's name, the one she had mostly gone by all her life in order to avoid people knowing she was born a part of the Gorgonio mob family.

"Uh...Janis. Janis Davos."

"And you are...?"

"I'm helping. I'm sort of an assistant. Trying to keep him calm. I know any sort of movement can be so dangerous for him." Her voice was shaking with her fear for his safety and she stopped for a moment, embarrassed. "He doesn't want to take anything that will make him drowsy, so I'm just trying to keep him from hurting himself."

"Really?" The queen's voice was all sympathy. "How long have you known him?"

"Uh... Actually..."

Janis drew in a shuddering breath. She couldn't lie to the queen! "It's sort of a strange situation. You see, he has this amnesia thing and so he doesn't remember me. But we knew each other quite well and..."

"Say no more," Pellea said as though she understood everything that was still unspoken. "I get the picture and I trust you. I can hear your honesty in your voice. I want you to come to the castle with him."

"Oh, Your Highness..." That was something she hadn't expected.

"And call me Pellea. I know we're going to be good friends."

Call me Pellea. This was the Queen of Ambria talking to her like this. She was touched and grateful. "Oh, I hope so."

"I'll get the medics ready to roll. Someone will call when they are on their way."

"Thank you so much."

She rang off and turned to go to Mykal, but Kylos was standing just a few feet away, glaring at her and her heart jumped.

"So you knew him before, did you? I knew there was something fishy about you. Why keep it a secret? What's your angle?"

Mentally, she shook herself. It wasn't easy making the transition from the queen's kind generosity to Kylos's feral animosity.

She looked toward the bedroom. She really wanted to go in and see about Mykal. "It's a long story and I…"

He grabbed her arm, fingers digging in. "You're a lying little thief, aren't you?"

She looked up into his face. She had the urge to send him sprawling again, but she resisted it. "No. No, I swear, I didn't really lie, I just let you think things that weren't true."

"Oh, really! I'm afraid the subtlety of that distinction is somewhat lost on me, darling." He squeezed her flesh painfully. "I want an explanation and I want it now."

Giving him back as fierce a glare as he was giving her, she began to peel his fingers off her arm, one at a time. "I have to check on your brother first. Then I'll fill you in on the background to this. I swear."

He grabbed her chin in his other hand, holding it roughly. "You'd better keep that promise. I'll give you exactly ten minutes and if you don't meet me back here, I'll tell Mykal what a lying little rat you are."

And then, to her surprise, he let her go. As she hurried back to the bedroom, she couldn't help but wonder at his motives. He must want to know her story awfully badly to bargain with her like this. And the way he'd said it implied he wasn't planning to kick her out— at least not yet.

But was he going to tell Mykal? Maybe yes, maybe no.

Mykal looked drained but recovering his strength. He gave her a crooked smile as she came in and began fussing around him. "Who was on the phone?" he asked as she poured him a glass of water.

She flashed him a brilliant smile. "The queen. She wants you there at the castle as soon as possible."

"Oh." He grimaced, looking unhappy. "And what if I decide not to go?"

"What?" She stared at him, aghast. "Why wouldn't you want to go?"

He met her gaze for a long moment and finally he confessed. "I'm not sure I want to be a prince," he said.

CHAPTER SIX

JANIS caught herself and held back the cry of dismay that came quickly to her lips. "But…" She swallowed hard. "Mykal, if you are one of the royal DeAngelis family, you can't pretend you're not. The DNA doesn't lie. If the final judgment says you're a prince, you're a prince. You don't get to pick and choose, do you?"

"Imprisoned by my bloodline. Is that the way it goes?"

She bit her lip, thinking how that statement could apply to her as well as to him. She'd been trapped by her family's past and she'd worked hard to put it behind her, only to have it crop up again and again.

But that background was criminal and she'd known it could ruin her chances of a decent life. This was so different. His true

ancestry could transform his life into something so wonderful. But obviously, that wasn't
the way he was looking at it.

"I'll make the decision on what I want to
do with my future," he said simply. "I don't
have to accept a life I don't want."

"But here in Ambria…"

"That's just it. I don't have to stay here in
Ambria. The rest of the world doesn't give a
damn about princes from Ambria. I can go
somewhere else."

He was right, of course. This was his decision and if he didn't want to be a prince,
what right did anyone have to make him do
it anyway? None.

In some ways, she was torn. If he accepted
the royal position, she knew he would be lost
to her forever. Even if he didn't she didn't
have much hope with him. But everything
in her yearned for his success and happiness,
and she had a feeling he shouldn't pass up this
chance.

"Fair enough," she said at last. "But I would
just say one thing. They have wonderful medical care at the castle and that is what you
need right now. It wouldn't hurt to get opin-

ions from the best physicians in the country." She sighed. "And Queen Pellea seemed so nice." She gave him a halfhearted grin. "And anyway, since they want you, why not at least give them a shot at convincing you? It can't hurt. If it's not meant to be, you'll find a way to turn it down gracefully, I'm sure of it."

He stared at her and she couldn't tell if he'd really been listening. She bent down to fluff his pillows and he reached up and sank his fingers into her hair, letting go easily as she straightened again, watching her hair pour out of his grasp as though it were liquid gold. She looked at him, wide-eyed. He'd loved playing with her hair in the past. Did he remember, even a little bit? The feel of his touch made her shiver.

"I cannot begin to express to you how much I hate this," he said absently, as though half his attention was still on her hair.

"Hate what?" she asked quickly.

"Not being able to get around by myself." His gaze met hers. "Depending on other people just to walk in the yard."

"Have some patience," she said, shaking her head. "You came in here on a gurney not even fifteen hours ago. You can't get up and dance. Not yet."

His eyes were hard as they looked into hers. "Will you dance with me, Janis?" he asked softly. "When I can dance again, I want you for my partner."

Her pulse began to race. He was half-teasing, playing with her for his own amusement. Little did he know how she wished he really was serious about it.

"I will," she told him earnestly. "If you still want me."

She loved him so. Might as well admit it. That hadn't changed and she didn't think it ever would.

She'd loved him from the moment she first saw him. She knew very well that the whole concept of love at first sight was ridiculous. She didn't believe in it. You couldn't really love someone you didn't know. So she wasn't sure just what that was that had grabbed her the first time her eyes had met Mykal Marten's.

There was no doubt she'd been blown away. After all, he was incredibly good-looking. His dark hair was cut short but it still managed to curl around his head, reminding her of a statue of an ancient Greek Warrior. His body was warriorlike, too—hard and muscular and broad in all the best places. His eyes were pale, pale blue, like spring flowers, but burning with a hard, fearless light that seemed to blaze out from those gorgeous thick eyelashes.

All in all, her heart had stopped in her throat and for a moment, she thought she'd never breathe again. Maybe that wasn't love, but it was something. It had almost seemed like some sort of force field had sprung between them, electric and throbbing, like a beat at a really hot dance club.

One look and she knew—he was the one.

Had he felt the same? Maybe. Maybe a little. But she didn't think it had happened to him in quite the same full-throttle way. Still, she'd let him know how she felt from the first. She had no choice. It was as though she needed the breath from his lips to survive.

Now was no different. She would do anything to bring their relationship back to the way it had been. Anything.

And that was her misfortune, because she

knew nothing would work. The longer she stayed near him, the more she realized that. Roadblocks were piling up, one after another. It was no use. She'd made up her own mind. She couldn't go to the castle with him. This would be a final goodbye. She turned away, afraid he would see the tears shimmering in her eyes.

"I'll just go refill this with water," she said, blinking rapidly as she took the porcelain pitcher and turned toward the door. "And I think I'll see if Griswold has made some breakfast for you. I'll be right back."

"Janis, wait a minute," he said, stopping her. "Could you do me a favor?"

She turned back slowly, keeping her face averted. "Of course."

"There's something I've got to do. If you look in the desk in the study, I think you'll find some writing paper and a fountain pen. I'd like to send a note to my parents. I know they'll be affected by all this royal speculation when they hear about it and I want to reassure them that I'm still their son."

She smiled, loving him, loving his decency. "Of course," she said, turning to look at him and barely able to resist the urge to throw her arms around him and give him a hug. "Just give me a few minutes."

He nodded, closing his eyes, and she left quickly, hoping to make quick work of her meeting with Kylos and do the chores for Mykal at the same time.

The study was empty. She found the desk quickly and pulled open one drawer after another until she found the paper Mykal had asked for. She drew the whole packet out and chose two sheets, then looked down, about to put it back. But an official-looking form on the bottom of the drawer caught her attention and she stopped to glance at it, feeling slightly nosy, but interested.

It was a death certificate. That gave her a start, but once she'd read the name on it, as well as the date and place of death, she was even more shocked. This had to be Mykal's adoptive father. She couldn't ignore that and she reached down to bring it up, immediately noticing another death certificate, this one for his mother, right under it. She read them over quickly, noting they both seemed to have died in a traffic accident, then heard Kylos coming down the hallway.

Moving as fast as she could, she put back the two documents and placed the packet of paper back where it had been, then closed the drawer just as Kylos entered the room. Turning, she stared at him. His parents had passed away and he hadn't told Mykal. At least, that was certainly what this looked like. What on earth could be his motive? Should she challenge him on it? Or just add it to the list of things she didn't trust about him?

But Kylos had his mind on other things.

"Okay, let's hear it," he said, facing off in front of her like a prizefighter. "Give it to me straight or you're going out on your ear."

She looked at him and wondered why he gave off such bad vibes. She really didn't like him much. Why did he want to know all this and what did he plan to do with the information? There was no doubt she had better be careful in what she told him.

"Mykal and I met a good six months ago. We were both in the military, still wrapping up war business in a way, and we worked together on a couple of assignments."

"The war is over," he said caustically, as though that somehow invalidated her story.

She rolled her eyes. "The war is not over. Sure, there's a truce of sorts between the royals and the Granvilli side. The Granvillis think they run one small, mountainous part of the island. But things there are falling apart and the royals are just biding their time. They'll take over soon."

"'They'?" He smirked. "So you fought on the side of the Granvilli murdering traitors?"

She winced. Just whose side had she been on when the Granvilli secret police had thrown her into the prison camp? "What does it matter anymore?" she said softly.

"It matters a lot to those of us who are loyal." But he said it in a pro forma way that let her know he really didn't care all that much. He'd gone on to something else and he frowned, thinking it over. "But that means Mykal was there, too, on the wrong side. Is that right?" He stared at her. The light of something eager gleaming in his eyes. "Was my brother a traitor?"

She shook her head, but before she could say anything, he went on, frowning. "So that's why I'm having so much trouble getting any records of his service out of our military bureaucracy. The royals asked me to get together all his history and papers and I've been having a hard time. But I'm asking the wrong side for info." He shook his head as though thoroughly confused. "And that's why no one could find him for the last two years. He was with the enemy. Who knew?"

She sighed. "It's more complicated than that and you're going to have to ask Mykal to explain it. I can't."

Kylos stared at her for a moment, then snapped his fingers. "Double agent. Am I right?"

"Ask him."

He scowled. "You know I can't do that right now. We can't do anything that might upset him. And anyway, he claims he can't remember anything." His gaze sharpened. "Are you buying that?"

"You mean, do I think he's telling the truth?" she asked, incredulous. "One thing about Mykal," she added coldly, "he's not like the rest of us. He never lies."

"Wow, you really have been brainwashed, haven't you?"

She shrugged and threw her hands out, starting to turn away, but he stopped her.

"Okay, you haven't finished. Tell me more."

She couldn't hold back the long-suffering look. "About what?"

"You and my brother. Come on. Lay it on the line. What's the story?"

She hesitated, but she knew she would have to comply, at least with some sort of sketchy outline of the truth. He'd overheard what she'd told the queen and she couldn't go back on that. "Well, we became quite close."

"Really." He gazed at her levelly. "Was the word *love* bandied about?" he asked with some sarcasm.

She drew in breath through her nose while she considered what to say to that. He didn't have to know they had actually married. No one had to know about that. At least, not until she and her baby were long gone.

"Sure," she said at last. "A time or two."

Something flared in his eyes and then they narrowed. "Sounds just peachy. There's nothing like a good love story to touch the heart."

He snorted his derision at the concept. "But then there was trouble in paradise, wasn't there? What happened?"

"We…we had a pretty bad fight a little over two months ago. We broke up and I hadn't seen him since. I came by yesterday to…to…"

He grunted. "You were hoping to patch things up, weren't you?"

"Yes. No." She grimaced in frustration. "Actually I just wanted to tie up some loose ends. I didn't know about the accident. I had no idea about the injuries. So I was shocked when the ambulance arrived and when everyone assumed I was here to take care of him, I let them believe it."

"Sure," he said, sounding as though he didn't buy a word of it. "And hearing about the royal thing didn't have anything to do with it. Right?"

"It didn't."

His mouth twisted cynically. "But it sure must have pricked up your ears once you heard about it, huh?"

She despised the man. How dare he impugn her motives like this? She had enough to be ashamed of, she didn't need to regret things she hadn't even done. "No, honestly, I didn't know a thing about it."

"Be serious," he said scornfully. "It's been all over the news."

"I hadn't heard any news. I've been... away."

His gaze narrowed. "What's your game, Janis Davos? What is it that you really want here?"

Her chin rose and she looked him in the eye. "I want Mykal to be safe and healthy and happy."

"That's it?"

"Yes."

"Bull."

"It's true. When I got here, I was all set to meet with him. I didn't know he had amnesia until I was talking to him and realized..." Janis shivered, remembering, and suddenly most of the fight went out of her. "It's just so crazy," she said weakly.

"So he doesn't remember you at all?"

She shook her head. "No."

Kylos nodded, thinking that over. "Why haven't you told him who you really are?"

She shrugged. "I expected him to know

the minute he saw me. But when that didn't happen, I'd already been told he wasn't supposed to get too physical or too emotional. And after the fight we had…well, I had to hold off. I couldn't tell him."

He gave her a completely skeptical look. "You're lying."

"No, I…"

"You heard about him maybe being the lost prince and you came running back to cash in on some of that glory. Am I right?"

She glared at him. "No, you are not right."

"Then why haven't you told him who you are?"

In order to explain that, she would have to tell him about the marriage and how she'd destroyed it with her own foolish actions. She couldn't do that. Instead, she went on the offensive herself.

"I've already gone over all that. And you have a thing or two to explain, yourself." She used an index finger to poke at his chest as she made her points. "Why haven't *you* told him the truth about your parents? Why haven't you told him that your parents have passed away?"

Kylos's dark face registered shock at that. He looked visibly shaken and he took a step backward, away from where Janis stood. "What? What are you talking about?"

"I saw the death certificates." She gestured toward the drawer in the desk. "Mykal just told me a few minutes ago that he wants to write a letter to them. So he obviously doesn't know. Why haven't you told him the truth?"

He was backing away now. "You know why. He can't take the shock. It could kill him."

"That's your story and you're sticking to it, huh?" She glared at him. "That excuse sounds a lot like mine, doesn't it? Funny how you didn't buy it when it was coming from me."

He muttered something but she wasn't listening.

"It looks to me like we have a standoff," she announced, hands on her hips. "You keep your secret and I'll keep mine. Okay?"

He appeared defiant, then grudgingly agreeable. "Okay. For now. We'll see." Then his eyes narrowed and his confidence seemed to return. "In the meantime, I'm going to look into your background, Janis Davos. Why do

I have a sneaky little suspicion that you have things to hide?" His dark eyes glittered maliciously. "Who can I talk to about you? Anyone at the castle?"

Hoping he was just trying to shake her, she fought back with sarcasm. "I don't know. Why not try Queen Pellea? She seems to be my best friend there."

Moving forward, he grabbed her arm, twisting it painfully. "Listen, you little tramp," he began, but the sound of someone clearing his throat in the doorway stopped him cold and he pulled away from her.

They both turned to see Griswold trying to look as though he hadn't seen a thing out of order.

"Your visitors are here, Mr. Marten," he said formally. "Perhaps you had better come and see to them."

"Oh." He headed for the door, leaving her behind, and she breathed a sigh of relief, rubbing her arm and watching as Griswold turned away with barely a glance at her.

Kylos was a real problem. She knew she shouldn't be goading him. She was probably going to regret it. But he was so obnoxious, she couldn't help herself. Turning on her heel, she made her way back to the room where Mykal was.

She'd forgotten all about the water pitcher and breakfast, but luckily, Griswold had already brought him a plate of eggs and fried potatoes and he was eating with gusto.

That made her feel better instantly. He would get healthy again, she was sure of it. She settled back to watch him eat and listen to him talk about simple things that needed little or no response. He seemed to have forgotten about writing a letter to his adoptive parents, and she didn't want to remind him. How sad and awkward that would be. But he seemed so free and easy, she could almost fool herself into thinking this was like the old days as she laughed at some silly joke he'd made. And then something would remind her that her heart was broken and she would lose the glow for a moment or two. But all in all, she just loved being with him.

She took the used plates to the kitchen and was surprised to see Kylos ushering a nice-looking older couple down the stairway. But she was hardly shocked when he treated her like a servant in front of them, leading them away quickly to another side of the house. What a strange one he was.

The castle called. An ambulance had been scheduled and would soon be on its way. A castle physician called and suggested that Mykal take his pain medication before making the trip to guard against jostling that was bound to happen. He made a face but accepted the pills with good grace once she'd explained the reasoning behind it.

"Okay," he said. "Just one more time. After this, it's going to take a stake through my heart to get me to take any more."

She counted out a dose and gave it to him. He washed it down with water and looked at her with sad eyes.

"I'm ready for this to be over and done with," he told her. "I'm going to give my permission to go ahead and operate. Let the surgery begin."

That startled her. "No," she said anxiously. "Wait until you get a proper evaluation before you make up your mind. Don't make any rash decisions now."

"Why not?" he said cynically. "What have I got to lose?"

"Everything!"

Looking at her, he grinned and before she realized what he was doing, he'd reached out and taken her hand, pulling her closer. "Okay, my beautiful guardian. I'll take your word for it." Bringing her hand to his lips, he kissed her in a courtly fashion, then looked up earnestly. "And anyway, you'll be there to help me make the right choice."

Slowly, she shook her head. "I don't think I should go to the castle with you," she said breathlessly.

"But I thought you worked for the castle."

"Not really. I'm…" What was she exactly? What could she say? Suddenly, she wanted to tell him the truth.

"Hey, how's this?" He pulled her hand to his chest. His eyes sparkled with something close to his old charm. "I command you to come with me."

She looked into those eyes for a moment, then rolled her own, half-laughing. "Oh, brother."

"You can't defy me."

"Oh, yeah? Watch me."

He pretended to frown fiercely. "We have dungeons for people like you."

"Only at the castle. Where I'm not going."

"Of course you're going." He thought that over for a moment, then gave her a disgruntled look. "What good is it going to be being royal if I can't throw my new power around?"

She smiled, loving him. "Maybe being royal isn't all its cracked up to be these days," she teased. "Maybe you're going to have to get used to some limits." And just to show him that she had some of her own, she slipped her hand back out of his and moved a little farther from the edge of the bed.

It wouldn't be long before the ambulance arrived. And then she would have to make good on her decision not to go to the castle with him. It was really the only choice. They couldn't go on like this. She couldn't live this lie any longer. She only hoped she could stay strong and determined enough to follow through with it. In the meantime, she began to look at him for evidence the pain medication was working. He wasn't acting as though anything was bothering him much, but she didn't notice him getting sleepy, either.

"How are you feeling?" she asked him.

"Stiff. My back is aching, but not as badly as it was earlier."

"Are you getting drowsy?"

He grimaced. "A bit. It's coming on. Don't worry."

"I just want you to be comfortable on the trip," she reminded him.

He nodded, but his mind was obviously on something else. He searched her face. "So how did you become a guard, Janis?"

She hesitated, but decided to try to get closer to the truth if that was possible. "I'm not really a guard. This assignment just kind of fell into my lap."

He nodded. "I have a feeling you did some military work during the war. Am I right?"

Her breath caught in her throat. Could he be beginning to remember? "Yes."

"Special forces? Or intelligence?"

She laughed, shaking her head. "Why would you think that?"

"Instinct. The kind of things you say. The way you handled Kylos. The way you look at me, as though you know what I'm thinking before I think it."

She smiled. "So you think I can read minds?"

He shrugged. "I wouldn't put it past you." He raised an eyebrow. "So am I right?"

She nodded slowly.

"Good. Then you are just the woman I need."

"Really? In what way?"

"Talent and training. I have something I'd like you to do for me."

"What is that?"

He met her gaze with his own and stared hard. "I want you to find my wife for me."

Her heart stood still, then raced so hard she thought she would keel over. "Uh…did you remember getting married?" she asked breathlessly.

He shook his head. "No. But it seems I did." He gestured toward a wooden box sitting on the dresser. "They gave me all the effects I was carrying with me when I was brought in, after the accident. I finally took a look at it a few minutes ago. You look, too— you'll see what I mean."

Rising, she went to the box and opened it. Inside she saw his wallet, his keys and his wedding ring. Their wedding ring. Her heart began to pound. She turned to look at him.

"You were wearing this ring in the accident?" she asked. That didn't seem reasonable. They had exchanged rings in their wedding, but they only wore them at home, when they were alone. Their wedding had been a secret that could have resulted in them both being fired from their jobs if they'd been found out. And after the fight they'd had, after what he'd said, why would he have been wearing the ring? She stared at him, completely at sea.

He shrugged. "So it seems."

"But…" She pressed her lips together to keep from saying something she would regret.

"Kylos doesn't know anything?" She only asked in order to see what he would say.

"No. We didn't have much contact over the last couple of years." He shrugged. "At least, not that I remember." He looked into her eyes. "You're wondering where my wife is, aren't you?" he said sensibly. "I don't know. I feel like something must have happened. That's why I want you to find her."

She was numb. What on earth could she say to that? "What if she doesn't want to be found?" she murmured, then wished she hadn't.

"You've got a point," he said, looking sleepy. "If she still wanted me, she would have shown up by now, wouldn't she?"

"Oh! Not necessarily. Maybe she doesn't know what happened."

"Maybe." He flexed his back and grimaced at the pain. "There are a lot of screwy things going on with this whole issue. For instance—look at the ID in the wallet."

She pulled the wallet out and opened it, but she already knew what it would say. There it was, a picture of Mykal, and the name John Blunt on the card. John Blunt. It was a name she knew well. It was the name he'd been going by as he infiltrated a local shipbuilder's union in the small seaside city of Pierria where they had both been working undercover.

So Mykal had been racing down a road on that old rattletrap motorcycle he loved with his John Blunt identity card in his pocket and the wedding ring he owned as Mykal Marten on his finger. It didn't make any sense.

"When was your accident?" she asked him, her mind working a mile a minute. "Where was it? Do you know?"

He shook his head. "About two months ago. And somewhere in Granvilli territory, from what I've been told. But I don't know where exactly."

She stared at him. Certain things were beginning to put up little red flags in her thinking. "How did they find your real identity?"

"It took a while. I was in a Granvilli hospital for a few weeks, I guess, and then I got transferred to the royal side in a prisoner trade. It seems they figured out I was a spy for the royals." His smile was endearingly crooked, but getting more and more sleepy. "I only wish I could remember. It sounds like I was living quite the life over there."

"Yes," she said softly, holding the memories close. "You were." She stared at him for a long, trembling moment. This had gone on long enough. Her resistance was melting. He had to know the truth.

But he didn't seem to notice what she'd said. He shook his head as though to clear it and looked at her through squinted eyes. "So will you help me?" he asked, his voice getting slurred. "I just have this aching void inside, and I feel like, if I could find her, if I knew who she was, I could fill this emptiness. And maybe find a reason to care whether I survive these operations or not."

"Oh, Mykal."

She went to him. She couldn't help it. She slipped right onto the bed beside him, being careful not to put any pressure on him in any way, but taking his face between her hands and kissing him firmly on the lips.

He kissed her back and she clung to him, so hungry for his affection, so thirsty for his taste. It was heaven to hold him.

But she had to pull away so that she could tell him the truth.

"Mykal," she said softly, touching his beloved face with the palm of her hand and looking into his eyes. "I know where your wife is. I'm so sorry I didn't tell you right away." She took a deep breath and plunged in. "I'm...I'm the one. It's me. You and I were married about four months ago."

He was staring at her but his eyes were blank. She bit her lip, disturbed by his lack of reaction. Frustrated, she leaned her head back on the pillow and stared at the ceiling as she talked. She couldn't look at him. She didn't want to see growing awareness in his eyes as he listened to her.

"We met in Pierria. We both worked there. I was with the Granvilli intelligence, and you were...well, I never understood exactly who you worked for or why. But we fell in love. Crazy in love. And we got married on a wing and a prayer, hardly knowing what we were doing. And then..."

She took a deep breath and closed her eyes. "And then we had a terrible fight. I ran from our little house to my brother's apartment. And I never saw you again." She opened her eyes and turned to look at him. "Until yesterday, when I..."

Her voice faded away as she realized he was asleep.

"Mykal!" she cried, but he didn't budge. She stared at him and then she began to laugh until tears filled her eyes. Here she'd painfully revealed it all to him, and he wasn't even listening. "Oh, Mykal."

She rose from the bed and looked down at him, shaking her head. She heard voices out in the foyer. The ambulance had arrived. They'd come to take him to the castle.

Well, things had changed. She'd said she was leaving, but now she was going to stay with him. This was her husband and he needed her. There was no way she was going to stay behind.

She picked up her satchel and turned, looking at the wooden box. Should she take it along? She didn't like leaving it here. But did she have the right?

"Nuts," she said to herself. She was married to the man. Of course she had the right. Moving quickly, she opened her satchel and put the box inside it. She'd barely completed the move before Kylos came rushing in the room and stopped abruptly as he saw her fastening her satchel.

"What are you doing?" he asked suspiciously.

"Getting ready to go to the castle," she said,

trying hard not to look guilty. For a second, she thought he was going to ask her to empty out her bag so he could take a look at what she had in there. But the moment passed and he turned to look at Mykal.

"Where's the medication?" he asked her. "How much is left?"

"It's in the bathroom," she said, frowning. "I don't think he'll need it. They'll surely prescribe their own preferences once they examine him."

"Hmm." He looked at her sideways, then disappeared into the bathroom at the same time the paramedics appeared in the doorway.

She turned to look at Mykal. This was it. Who knew what would happen once they got to the castle? She took a deep breath and said a little prayer. It was time to go.

CHAPTER SEVEN

"THE first thing you're going to do," Queen Pellea said as she swept into the personal royal library where she'd told Janis to meet her, "is tell me all about my brother-in-law, the new prince." She took Janis's hands in hers and beamed at her. "Tell me everything you know."

Janis held on as though she were a life raft. She was overwhelmed by it all—the gorgeous castle, the sumptuous décor, the beautiful queen who looked like she'd stepped right out of a Renaissance painting. She'd helped bring Mykal in and she'd even had a chance to talk to one of the doctors about his symptoms over the last few hours. And then she'd received the message from the queen and had hurried here for a meeting.

"So you're sure of it?" she asked, wide-eyed. "He is the lost prince?"

Pellea shrugged. "The wise men won't say as yet, but I'm sure of it." She smiled impishly. "I just peeked in at him in the examining room. There's no doubt in my mind."

Janis smiled back, but the mood that filled her heart was melancholy, because she knew what that meant. "You may have to talk him into it," she told the queen. "He's grumbling about loss of freedom and that sort of thing."

"Oh, don't you worry. We'll have him singing a different tune soon enough. I'll have Monte deal with him," she added, referring to her husband, King Monte, oldest brother of the new prince. "Come, let's sit down and talk."

Janis followed her to a pair of comfortable chairs situated in front of a wide stone fireplace.

"And I'll tell you the second thing we're going to do," Pellea went on, eyeing her askance. "We're going to get some decent clothes for you and get you out of that blue jumpsuit." She shuddered. "Is that a uniform for something?"

"Sort of." Janis drew in a shaky breath. She hadn't expected this question to come up so quickly. It threw her off balance. She couldn't lie to the queen—especially after looking into her calm, kind eyes.

"Where did you get it?"

Wishing she could disappear, she whispered, "Prison camp."

"What?" Pellea said, leaning toward her and frowning as though she hadn't heard.

"Prison camp," she said aloud. Might as well own it. "I've been in a Granvilli prison camp for the last two months. I just got out."

"Oh!" Pellea sank back into the chair and stared at her. "Oh, my."

Janis drew in a sharp breath. She'd known this would make all the difference. The queen had been anxious to meet with her, but now they would throw her out. And who could blame them? You couldn't let a recently released prisoner hang around in the castle. True, at least she'd been in a Granvilli camp, not one run by the royals. But still. Her heart sank. She should never have come here.

Even if the queen were ready to hear her side of things, what could she say? There was no easy excuse. She could still hear her brother Rolo's voice hissing in her ear, "You really screwed this one up, Janny. You botched things so badly, your own husband turned you in." But she couldn't tell Pellea about that.

If she got up and walked out right now, could she avoid the humiliation of being escorted out by an armed guard? She eyed the doorway nervously.

But, though shocked, Pellea wasn't through with her yet. "What on earth did you do to end up there?" she asked sternly.

Janis shrugged. Was there really any point in going on with this? Why didn't the queen just call for the guard and get it over with? She took a deep breath and decided to give it a try. It was the least she could do, she supposed.

"You have to understand what it's like in the Granvilli territory right now. Society is falling apart. Everything is in chaos. People are reacting out of fear and anger. I don't really know why I was arrested. And I don't know why they let me go when they did."

That much was true. She knew what had

angered Mykal, but she didn't think that had anything directly to do with the reason she was held. If he really had been the one to turn her in, what reason had he given them? She didn't have a clue.

Pellea frowned, searching her eyes. "You were never charged with anything?"

Janis made a face. "That would require a functioning court system. They don't have that over there at present." She hesitated, ready to get up and go. "I know this is a shock to you." She began to rise. "I should have told you before."

"No." Pellea's voice had the unmistakable tone of command. "Sit down right now and tell me all about it."

"But why would you believe anything I say?" she protested, trying to be realistic about it.

Pellea tossed her head. "Talk," she ordered firmly. "Start with what happened once you were arrested. Where did they take you and what did they tell you?"

That wasn't as easy to do as it might seem. Janis licked her lips, remembering her conversation with the warden and trying to think what she could tell the queen about it.

"What is my crime?" she'd cried desperately.

The warden had stared coldly. "Espionage."

Espionage. That was what they paid her to do. How could they arrest her for it? "What kind of espionage?"

The warden's gaze didn't waver. "Illegal espionage."

That was all she was ever told. She was taken to the makeshift camp near the border, stripped of all her clothing and possessions, along with her dignity, and given her blue jumpsuit to wear. The next two months had been a nightmare. The food was terrible but not plentiful, so hunger was more important than quality. She lost twelve pounds, but she wouldn't have recommended it as a diet experience. The work assignments were uniformly disgusting. And every night she had to fight off the prison guards. Luckily the army had given her some good basic self-defense moves and she held her ground, leaving the guards to go after easier pickings. But just the fact that she'd had to maintain that struggle night after night was enough to make her bitter.

What of all that could she tell the queen? But she had to tell her something and she tried. And she managed, haltingly, leaving out a few things, like the marriage, and her brother, and some of the seamier aspects of prison camp life. But all in all, she stayed pretty true to the real story line.

The queen listened impassively. "What was this espionage they arrested you for? You must have some idea of the catalyst."

She took a deep breath. Maybe she was ready to give a fuller picture of what she was involved with now that she'd told her this much. Maybe she could outline a hint of what Mykal had caught her doing that had led to his outrage.

"It was a surveillance report on things another agent had done," she said. "I…I made some copies and gave them to someone I thought I could trust." Why she'd done that for her brother was a story she couldn't get into. "But…" She stopped, fighting back tears as she remembered Mykal's face when he found out what she'd done. Shaking her head, she couldn't go on.

Pellea watched her for a long moment, making no move to comfort her in any way. "Well, that all sounds very spy-versus-spy, doesn't it?" she said in a cool voice at last.

"Something like that," Janis admitted, her voice choked.

"Janis, nothing personal, but you do realize I have a responsibility here. I must be the guardian of my people, the protector of all who are in this castle."

"Of course. I understand."

Pellea paused, then added, "I'm afraid I'm going to have to ask you to leave."

Janis nodded. That was what she expected, once her imprisonment was known. It would be even worse if they knew about her family background. She was ready to go. She only wished she could see Mykal once more before she left, though. She had a feeling that, once she left, she might never see him again.

They rose together and Janis turned away. She wanted to get this over with as quickly as possible. But she stopped, realizing she couldn't leave the room before the queen did.

Pellea came toward her, hand outstretched, looking ready to say goodbye, but a courtier was suddenly in the doorway.

"Your Majesty," he said, bowing deeply. "You are wanted in the hospital wing. Dr. Pheasar asks that you come to him immediately."

Pellea turned to Janis. "This must be about Mykal," she said. She stared at Janis for a moment, then reached out for her again. "You'd better come, too," she said, then turned without another word and hurried for the elevator.

Janis was right behind her. Had something happened to Mykal? Her heart was thumping and she was hurrying as they exited the elevator on the hospital floor, but she could hardly keep up with the queen. In a moment they were in the medical unit.

"No entry, please," the nurse said, jumping up to stop them, but then shrinking back when she saw who it was. "Oh, excuse me Your Majesty."

They rushed right through the barriers and finally they were in the examining room where the doctor was looking at X-rays in a computer screen. Mykal was still unconscious, covered in a sheet and lying on a table on the other side of the room. Janis looked from him to the doctor to the X-rays and back to Mykal again, hardly knowing what to think, but terrified of what they might hear.

"Take a look at this," the surgeon was saying, pointing to where tiny lines that looked like needles were scattered so very close to a section of Mykal's spinal column. "This is not good. I've conferred with a number of my colleagues and we have mixed opinions. But most of us think it's too dangerous to attempt any removal of the closest ones at this time. I'll be sending copies of their reports along with my own and you can read them for yourself. But I wanted you to see this." He turned and looked at them both. "He can still live a full and active life. But I'm afraid he will need to be confined to a wheelchair most of the time."

Janis drew her breath in with a gasp and Pellea frowned.

"I thought you told me initially that you felt the shards were too close to leave them," she said. "That they might move in and compromise his mobility on their own if left alone."

"Yes, that was what I thought before I got a look on my own. But examining this more closely makes me think we just can't risk it."

Pellea looked at Janis. "What do you think?" she asked her. "How will he take this news?"

Janis was startled to be asked for an opinion. But she had one. "If it were up to me," she said, head high and voice clear, "I would keep him as safe as possible. I wouldn't operate. I would wait and see." She looked at them both and shook her head. "But I know what he wants. And he couldn't stand a cossetted life. He'll choose surgery. You can count on it."

Pellea frowned, looked at the doctor and shrugged. "We'll talk again once he's awake and lucid," she said. Looking at Janis, she gestured for her to follow. "Come with me," she said.

Janis tried to do just that, but she couldn't. She had to turn and look at Mykal again, then go close and touch him, just for a quick second. This might be the last time she would see him. The second stretched out, and she leaned down to kiss his forehead. "I love you," she whispered, then straightened and turned to find Pellea watching her.

"I'm sorry," she said awkwardly. "I just couldn't leave."

Pellea didn't say a word, but turned and started down the hall, with Janis hurrying after her.

"I'd like you to come to my room for a moment," she told her as they boarded the elevator again. "We need to finish our talk."

Janis nodded and quickly found herself in a beautiful courtyard, with a greenhouse roof, open to the sky, that served as a sitting room. Exotic plants had turned the space into a barely controlled jungle. Brightly colored birds flew from plant to plant, and frogs croaked in a little stream that wound through the area.

"Sit," Pellea told her. "And tell me the rest of the story."

She sat. "What is it that you want to know?"

"I want to know who Mykal is. What sort of man. I understand I am going to have to learn these things on my own, but you can start the process by telling me how you met and why you were together."

Janis frowned, curious. "I'm sure you've researched him."

"Of course. We have a complete record of his activity up until a little over two years ago. Then the trail goes cold. And that is exactly the time he can't remember. So you see, it does become a bit of a problem."

"Oh. And you want me to fill you in."

"If you will, please."

But should she? Was the queen just going to use her for all the information she could gather, then throw her out into the street? Probably. But she realized she didn't have a lot of choice—unless she wanted to be a jerk. And she really didn't want that at all. So she nodded. "You know he was in the military."

"Yes. We've found the paperwork on his recruitment in the royal army two and a half years ago. But after that…nothing. We can't find anyone by that name in the service at all. And no one seems to be able to tell us anything."

Janis nodded. "That's because we were… I mean, he was recommended for intelligence work from the beginning. On the black side."

"The black side."

"That means he had volunteered to take training to do extreme espionage work. Only the most dangerous missions. And so they probably blotted out his identity right away. That way, if he was caught, no one would be able to trace him back to the command group."

Pellea nodded. "I see." She sighed. "And did he see much action?"

"During the war, yes. Once the truce was declared, the hot war turned cold and our assignments got a bit more ordinary." She smiled, remembering. "For a while I was actually going up and down streets, pretending to be a meter maid, but really checking who lived there. We did a lot of that sort of thing."

A tiny smile appeared in the queen's eyes. "Someone's got to do it."

"Unfortunately, that someone was me."

Pellea frowned. "But wait a minute. You were in the Granvilli military. Is that right?"

Here came the sticky part. "Yes. My family was based in Granvilli territory. It just seemed natural."

She waved the explanation away. "Of course. But what about Mykal?"

"When we met, he was in Granvilli intelligence, just as I was. And I assumed…"

"But he was actually working for us?"

She nodded. "Yes."

Pellea's smile was full this time. "That's a relief."

"But I didn't know that until later."

"So he was a double agent?"

She nodded, then shook her head, troubled. "You know, I don't feel right telling you things about Mykal. He should tell you himself."

Pellea looked frustrated. "But he can't. It's possible that he will never be able to remember what happened during the war. In the meantime, we have to be prepared for everything. And the only way that can happen, is if you tell us."

Janis thought for a moment, then looked up. "I have to ask him first. I'm sorry, but I just don't feel free to explain his life for him without his permission."

Pellea looked as though she were about to say something, then stopped herself. "Of course," she said instead. Then her gaze sharpened. "Tell me this. Who recruited you into intelligence service?"

She hesitated. Just how much of herself did she owe them?

"My brother," she admitted at last. "He wasn't in the service but he did contract work for them. And he thought I was a perfect match."

"Was he right?"

She bit her lip, considering. "Sort of. I enjoyed the work. But I wasn't particularly proud of it. Do you know what I mean?"

"You were good at it, but you weren't sure it was honorable."

She nodded. Pellea had hit the nail on the head. It was such a joy to talk to someone who understood so quickly. "Exactly."

"And Mykal?"

She couldn't help but smile. "He enjoyed it thoroughly. He loved putting things over on the bad guys, so to speak. He loved being smarter and more aware than other people."

"So playing a double game was right up his alley."

"Yes. So it seemed."

Pellea stared at her for a moment, then said,

"I can see that you love him. But tell me this. Do you like him?"

Janis laughed. "I adore him," she said with passion. "I love and admire everything about him. I would do anything for him."

Pellea thought for a moment, then said, "Janis, can you think of any reason why it would be dangerous for me or my family if you stayed here with us for a few days?"

Janis took the question seriously. She thought for a moment, then shook her head. "No."

"I don't have any documents you might want to copy," she said, half-teasing. "At least, not that I know of." She smiled. "In fact, I don't have any secrets at the moment. My life is an open book."

"Oh, Your Highness, that was such an anomaly. I would never…"

"Yes, yes, I'm sure of it. And I can tell you care deeply for Mykal. How he feels about you is a mystery, even to him." She smiled, touching Janis's cheek. "So I think you should stick around. He needs all the friends he can get right now."

Janis was overwhelmed. She hadn't expected this. "Your Royal Highness," she said, her voice cracking, "you're too kind."

"I'll have someone show you to a room you can use for the short term. And I'll make sure they let you know as soon as he is awake enough to see people."

CHAPTER EIGHT

MYKAL looked gaunt, like a Halloween version of himself. Janis leaned over the bed and put a hand on his chest to make sure he was breathing. He was. When he didn't react, she glanced around to make sure no one was lurking in the hallway, then leaned down and kissed his lips.

His eyes shot open and he smiled at her.

"Wow," he said faintly. "That wasn't a dream?"

She kissed him again, just to prove it, and he kissed her back.

"Did you find my wife?" he asked as she drew back.

She hesitated, looking down at him. He didn't remember. Or maybe he'd never heard a word she said. Should she say it again? She frowned. No. Not now. Once things were settled and secure, that would be the time.

"I've got a good strong lead on it," she said instead. "I'll tell you about it later."

He nodded, not taking his eyes off her. "Okay. I'll trust you."

That took away her smile and made her anxious again. He couldn't trust her. That was just the problem they had between them. What she wanted more than anything was to make things so that he could trust her again.

The surgeon came in and turned on the computer monitor to show Mykal the X-rays and Janis melted into the background, leaving them alone. She knew what they were discussing and she also knew she would have no say in the outcome. Pellea came by, gave her a hug and went on into the room. Janis watched through the window as she talked animatedly to the other two.

Suddenly a man appeared in the doorway, the sort of man who had a presence about him, the sort of man who made you step back a bit and stare in awe.

"Your Majesty," the nurse said, jumping up and dipping her head.

"Good evening," he replied in a friendly but distracted manner. He gave a faint smile to Janis as well as he walked on into the recovery room. She stared after him, sure this must be King Monte, Mykal's oldest brother. Now that she'd seen the king, she knew why Pellea had been so sure Mykal was a prince. They looked very much alike.

The king joined in the discussion. Mykal sat propped up with pillows and looking very determined.

Finally, she caught a sentence or two.

"We can operate first thing in the morning, if you're sure," the surgeon said.

Monte said something to Mykal, and then reached down take his brother's hand. It was an emotional moment. Janis had tears in her eyes as the king swept through again, avoiding her gaze as he left the area. She looked at Mykal and saw that he was blinking himself.

Pellea came out and smiled at her. "Go in and talk to him," she said. "They will try to remove the shrapnel first thing in the morning. That's his decision. I only pray that they are successful."

Janis went in and looked at him.

"So I guess it's true. You are royal."

"Ya think?"

They grinned at each other, and then his eyes sharpened as he looked her over.

"Hey. You look really pretty."

"Queen Pellea rustled up some clothes for me." She twirled in front of him, showing off the cute short skirt and the gauzy top. He smiled approvingly, but then a strange expression came over him. His gaze seemed to cloud over, as though he were remembering something. She waited, holding her breath, but he smiled again. Still, she could have sworn there was a hint of recognition, even for just a moment.

And then Kylos came barging into the room. "What the hell is this about operating on your back?" he demanded. "I don't think you should do it. Not yet."

"What are you doing here?" Mykal asked him.

"Talking to you. Trying to talk sense into you."

"No, I mean here at the castle."

"Oh. I asked to come. I thought you could use the moral support."

"No kidding?" Mykal met Janis's gaze and grinned.

She grinned back. Kylos went on talking, trying to convince Mykal to hold off on the operation but never making any real sense. And Janis and Mykal ignored him.

"What do you think?" he asked her. "Have you changed your mind?"

"I guess we'll follow your instincts and hope for the best," she told him. "I just want what will leave you safe. That's the most important thing to me."

His eyes darkened. "Why do you care so much?" he asked her. "You hardly know me."

She tried to smile. "I know you better than you think."

He nodded slowly. "We knew each other during my lost period, right?"

She nodded, trembling slightly and waiting for the hard questions. He studied her for a long moment, then smiled, and the hard questions didn't come.

"Have you got a date?" he asked her instead.

"A date?" She laughed. "Not yet."

"I mean, do you have something to do to-night?"

She shook her head, looking as him questioningly.

"Then how about staying with me for a while?" he asked simply. "I'm really feeling dopy and I'm probably going to fall asleep soon. But if you could stay with me until that happens…"

"It would be my pleasure." She sat down in the chair, feeling a rosy glow of happiness like she hadn't felt in a long time. "Anything you want."

He stretched back and began to talk, telling her about his childhood, about the parents who'd raised him with so much love and kindness, about his vacations at the beach. She listened and enjoyed finding out things about him she'd never known. She only wished she could have told him about their life together. Short as it was, it had been a joy. And it had resulted in a baby. She cupped her hands around her child and wondered if he would ever know about him or her. Too many unknowns littered their future. It was hard to tell which way the wind would blow from this vantage point. But whatever happened, she knew she would always love Mykal. If only she could count on him feeling the same.

The day seemed hectic. There was so much going on in the castle, it seemed like a small city, set up vertically instead of on the horizontal. Everyone she passed in the halls seemed to be bustling with a sense of urgency, on their way to do important tasks in interesting places. There was a certain electric excitement in the air. She liked it. She wandered about and gazed at everything as though she were at Disneyland.

But it was hard to immerse herself into any one thing. She couldn't erase the worry and push what was happening in that operating room out of her mind.

She'd been there when Mykal had woken in the morning. She'd kissed him again before she left, knowing it must be a bit confusing to him to have the woman he thought he'd tasked with finding his wife seeming so affectionate. But she couldn't help it. As soon as she could, she would tell him the truth, and this time she would make sure he was awake when she did it.

Still, that wasn't going to make the difference where the future of their relationship was concerned. Their marriage was doomed. She hoped and prayed that his operation would be successful, that he wouldn't be damaged, that he would be free to take his position in the royal family and enjoy it to the fullest. Everything should be perfect for him. He so deserved it.

She'd forgiven him in her heart for not coming to rescue her from the prison camp. It was her fault, after all. That day when he'd told her he could never trust her again had been the worst of her life. When the secret police had shown up to take her away, she'd almost felt she deserved whatever they might do to her.

But later, she began to wonder how it had come to that. After all, Mykal wasn't a die-hard Granvilli supporter. He was actually a secret royalist. So why would he have turned her in to the Granvilli authorities? It didn't make any sense.

But that hardly mattered anymore. Mykal

was a part of the royal family and that was something she could never be. It wasn't as though the family she came from was just some run-of-the-mill crime family. The Gorgonios defined organized crime in Ambria and had for over a hundred years. They were part of a dynasty, a sort of royalty of its own milieu. Her grandfather, her father and her uncle had been the rulers of the organization, each in turn. And each had been the most hated and wanted criminal in his time. There was no getting around it. She came from people who were scum.

She had tried to distance herself from her family in every way she could and she'd tried to get Rolo to join her. When he was younger, it had seemed to be working. Lately, she was afraid she was losing that struggle. She constantly tried to pull him away, and he just as stubbornly pulled back. He didn't seem to be able to make the commitment to leave organized crime forever.

She went into the library and picked out a couple of magazines, but she couldn't concentrate on the stories. And then she had a thought. Libraries kept old newspapers.

Maybe some paper they'd collected might have the news of Mykal's accident when the IED exploded. It was worth a try. So she spent a good hour looking through everything she would find that covered the first month after their separation. Nothing. She couldn't find a single item, and she was so disappointed, she had to get up and walk around the entire floor of the building to get her equilibrium back.

She visited the recreation center and considered playing a little table tennis, something she once had been good at. But she couldn't keep her mind on that, either. Her heart and her mind were in that operating room and there was no way to get around it.

At one point, she stopped into the royal breakfast room. Pellea had given her a pass. The tables were covered with a sumptuous feast of a breakfast spread. Everything looked delicious. But she knew she wouldn't be able to get anything down, so she made a short tour of the room, smiled at a couple of people who eyed her curiously and left again.

Outside, she went to a railing and looked down at the crowd in the halls on the floor below. And then she caught sight of something that chilled her blood, and she stepped back quickly so as not to be seen. Down below she saw her brother, Rolo, with her cousin Jasper. From what she knew of both those men, no one should have ever let them inside these castle walls. She began to walk, getting as far from them as she could. She could hardly breathe. What were they doing here? And what was she going to do about it?

Nightmare scenarios as to what they might be up to went swimming through her head, one after another. She knew she should tell Pellea about these two interlopers, but if she did, Pellea would find out quickly what sort of family she came from. She'd been gracious with her, but that would be a step too far for her to go. Rolo and Jasper would be sent packing—but so would she herself! And she couldn't go until she knew that Mykal was all right.

But not much longer than that. She had to leave before anyone knew she was pregnant. Of course, Mykal thought he knew already, but he wasn't going to tie it to her unless he got his memory back. And that was the abyss that yawned before her. They wouldn't want her once they found out about her ancestry. But they would want her baby.

A frantic wave of panic swept through her. No one must know. She would leave as soon as she could, go to the continent, maybe immigrate to Australia or Canada and take her baby as far from Ambria as she could get. She would get a false ID. She'd done that often enough in the past. She knew people who could help her. She had to go. No one must know.

She looked at her watch. Suddenly it was time to go back to the medical unit. She had to be as close to Mykal as she could get. It would be another hour or more before the surgeon would come out and give them the verdict, but she couldn't stay away any longer. Turning, she hurried to the elevators.

The waiting room was brightly painted and well-lit, but it seemed like the gloomiest place on earth to Janis. She sat in the plastic chair and flipped through a magazine, not even seeing the articles. Inside, she repeated a prayer over and over.

Please let him be safe. Please let him be safe.

It was impossible to sit still. She got up to pace, but as she passed the window to the nurse's station, she noticed the chair was empty. No one was manning the entryway. And that meant there was no one guarding the information.

Information—like files with background on a patient's health—or the details of the accident that had put him in the hospital in the first place. Should she? She stopped, thinking. Why not just ask to see them? But no. That never worked with people in charge of information. She would be told she had no standing. Better to try to do it on her own.

Gliding quickly, she went to the file cabinet and pulled open the drawer she thought should have Mykal's records. The folders were filed alphabetically and she began to search through them. She heard footsteps in the hall. She only needed another second or two.

The door opened and she was back pacing, but her heart was beating a mile a minute.

"Hello," the nurse said before dropping down into her seat behind the desk again.

"Hello," Janis said back. "I don't suppose you've heard anything?"

The nurse shook her head. "Sorry. I'll let you know as soon as I do."

"Thanks."

She went back to her chair and slumped into it, calming her heart rate and picking up her magazine. Mykal's folder hadn't been in the file drawer. She supposed it might be in the room where he was staying. At some point, she had to get hold of that file. It had become an obsession with her. She had to know.

She hadn't been there long before Kylos came sauntering into the room, dressed in black, as usual. She looked up and gave him a slight smile. She assumed his twitch was his answering salute. She went back to the magazine and he slipped into a chair beside her, looking just as tense as she felt.

"Have you heard anything?" he asked.

"No. Nothing." For a moment she thought they were going to have a bonding moment over the fate of his brother. He really seemed to care. A small wave that was almost affectionate went through her.

"I guess it was pretty much a surprise to you when he was told he was one of the lost princes," she commented.

"Not really," he replied, a pinch of bitterness in his tone. "Mykal always gets the gold ring. It seems to be his birthright."

"Yes," she said faintly. "I know what you mean."

"And what about you?" He leered at her. "How do you think someone like you is going to hang on to him?"

She blinked at him. "What do you mean?"

"I told you I was going to look into your background. I've already found out a few things."

Icy fingers traveled up and down her spine. "Like what?"

"Never mind." He leered again, acting as though he liked making her wait. "I'll talk to you about this later."

She shrugged, reminded of how annoying he was. But she couldn't think about her own problems right now. She had to worry about Mykal.

He moved restlessly. "What do you think? Is he going to die?"

She looked up, shocked. "No, he's not going to die! Where did you get such a ludicrous idea?"

He shrugged, looking uncomfortable. "I thought the shrapnel was pretty deep and pretty bad, and since they kept saying—"

"He's not going to die." She said it with passion, but she shivered deep inside. "What we're hoping for now is that he has no impaired motion. That his legs will work. That the operation won't leave him damaged in any other way."

Kylos frowned. "He probably won't be needing the pain medication anymore, huh?"

She stared at him, wondering at such a strange question. But then, Kylos was a strange man. "I have no idea."

He growled. "He shouldn't have done it."

"I'll tell you this. If this operation is successful and he comes out in good health and spirits, we're both going to tell him our secrets. Aren't we? I'm going to tell him who I really am and you're going to tell him about your parents. Right?"

"Are you crazy? He won't be ready to hear about that. Not for days." He shook his head and muttered, "Not for at least a few more days," but she had a feeling that wasn't really meant for her to hear.

"Kylos, do you have a job?"

"Of course I have a job. Well, I do contract work."

"What sort?"

He took a deep breath and let it out. "Okay, here's the deal. I went to law school. But the dean had it in for me so I never finished. But I got enough so that I can do some kinds of paralegal work. And that's what I do."

"Freelance?"

"Sort of. I've got a good friend, Leland Lake. He's an attorney and he hires me for various things."

She went back to her magazine. He moved nervously for a while, then got up to visit the restroom. Looking over at the seat, she noticed he'd left his mobile behind. And almost immediately, it rang.

She had to make a decision. His ring tone was awful, shrill and demanding. It seemed to echo off the waiting-room walls. It was way too loud. It had to be stopped.

Ordinarily she wouldn't answer someone

else's phone like this, but the noise was unbearable. Snatching it up, she flipped it on and said, "Yes?"

"Kylos Marten, please."

She recognized the voice. It was Griswold, the daily butler.

"He's not here right now, but this is Janis Davos. Hi, Griswold."

"Oh. Hello, miss."

"Can I give him a message?"

"Uh… Oh, well, why not? Please tell him that the party in question has arrived."

"Okay, Griswold, you're going to have to be a bit more specific. What party in question?"

He paused, then said, "The people interested in the house. He'll know what I mean. Tell him I will escort them about the grounds until he gets here, unless he calls and tells me differently."

"I see."

"Just tell him that. Thank you, miss."

Janis sat very still with her lips pressed together, thinking that over as she waited for Kylos to come back. And when he did, she waited until he had picked up his phone and began to take his seat.

"You had a call."

He reacted badly. "What! You answered it?"

"I had to stop the noise."

"That's not noise." He seemed quite offended. "That's my favorite band."

Rolling her eyes, she told him, "Griswold says the people interested in the house have arrived and he will go ahead and escort them about while waiting for you to show up." She frowned, gazing at him sharply. "What are you doing, selling the house?"

He didn't answer, but he gave her a furious scowl and bolted for the door. "I'll be back," he muttered as he disappeared.

Janis frowned after him. The little bugger was selling the house, and without talking to Mykal first. She had a very bad feeling about that. She didn't think Mykal was going to be happy when he found out. But of course, Mykal didn't know their parents had died. And here was Kylos, selling the house out from under him. That just wasn't right.

She went back to her magazine but she

couldn't even see the pictures anymore. *Please, please,* she kept chanting silently. *Make him be okay.*

It was already half an hour later than she'd been told it would be. Time seemed to be going in slow motion. Pellea looked in.

"Have you heard anything?" she asked.

Janis shook her head, feeling lost.

"I'll find out what's going on," the queen said, marching in through the double doors. And marching right back out again.

"No one's talking," she told Janis. "I'll be back a little later and see if I can get anything out of any of them."

Another half hour dragged by. Then another. She was up and pacing now, fear and panic chasing each other throughout her system. What could be wrong? Why wouldn't anyone tell her anything?

She'd tried going in to the operating room but a nurse had sent her back out. She was going crazy with worry.

Pellea came back to sit with her. She made a few calls on her mobile, trying to scare up some information, and finally she did get a scrap.

"They've sent for more experts from Vienna," she told Janis. "They sent for them quite some time ago and they are coming in as fast as they can get here."

"What does that mean?" Janis was as shaken as she'd ever been.

"I assume it means they've hit a problem. But don't worry. These guys are the best in the world."

Don't worry! She was nothing but worry. Any more and she would be lying in the corner in a fetal position, whimpering like a baby lamb.

But before she had time to really panic, they arrived, three of them, sweeping in through the waiting room and on into the operating theater like gods down from Olympus. Janis and Pellea stood holding each other, each whispering their own prayer. At one point, they heard shouting and Janis's eyes filled with tears.

"Oh, no!" she cried. "Something's happened to him."

"Hush," Pellea told her. "He'll be okay." But somehow her voice didn't have the conviction it had held earlier.

Another half hour passed. Kylos was back. When Janis introduced him to the queen, he was like a different man, all smiles and good manners. Janis could hardly believe the transformation, but she had no time to mull it over. She had to worry. If she didn't worry enough—superstition being what it was, she didn't know what would happen, but she knew she had to keep worrying. It was all she had left to do.

And then it was over. Dr. Pheasar came out, taking Pellea by the hands and shaking his head. Janis began to sob, but he looked up, surprised.

"No, my dear, don't cry. I think the prognosis is fairly good. Not perfect, but much better than I expected."

"Oh, doctor." Janis grabbed his arm. "Are you sure? Do you mean it?"

"Yes, I mean it. I think you'd better leave him alone tonight, but you should be able to go in and see him first thing in the morning."

Now she was really sobbing, and so was Pellea. But they were both laughing through their tears as well, looking at each other.

The doctor shook his head. "Women," he muttered.

But Janis didn't care. One hurdle had been crossed. Now all that was left was for Mykal to heal from the surgery—and get his memory back.

CHAPTER NINE

CLOSE to dawn, Janis slipped into Mykal's room and went right to his bed. Leaning over him, she kissed his lips and then she took his hand in hers. Slowly, he opened his eyes and looked at her. She waited nervously to see what her reception would be.

It was all that she could have hoped for. His smile was slow but it grew until his mouth was wide and his happiness reached his eyes. His gaze alone seemed to reach out and wrap her up for the keeping. Instinctively, he loved her. She could feel it. His head hadn't gotten the word yet, but his heart knew it.

"Hey," he said to her. "You're back. I've been waiting to see you."

"Me, too," she said simply. "We've got a lot to catch up on."

His smile wavered. "We did know each other before, didn't we?"

"Yes."

"I knew it. Funny how I can feel it, even though I can't remember it." He looked at her expectantly. "And...?"

She tried to smile was her nerves were getting the better of her. "First tell me how you feel."

"I feel great. I could practically get up and dance right now if I didn't have this damn IV stuck in my arm."

"None of that. You need to stay still and heal."

"Sure." He smiled at her, reassuring her again. "But, Janis, I'm going to be okay. I'm not going to have to spend my life walking around wondering if any slight little jostle will render me paralyzed." He shook his head. "You don't know what a relief that is."

"Oh, don't I?"

She smiled back at him and he searched her face, then reached out with his free hand and touched her cheek. She wanted to bury her face in his palm and kiss it, but she didn't dare do that. Not yet.

"Okay," he said, pulling back. "I've told you my news. You tell me yours." His eyes darkened slightly. "Did you find my wife?"

She nodded and she could tell her eyes were sparkling. Too bad she couldn't hold back the excitement she felt. It might just be her undoing. And yet she was about to tell him the truth. That had to be a good thing, no matter how he reacted. "Yes, I did."

He watched her, just barely holding back a smile. "Is it you?"

She nodded again.

His grin widened. "I had a feeling." Reaching out, he pulled her to him. "I knew it was going to be you." He hugged her a bit gingerly, using only one arm, but he breathed in the scent of her hair and shivered. "You couldn't have told me anything that would make me happier."

Janis laughed, full of joy. She ran the flat of her hand inside the opening of his hospital pajamas, caressing the chest she knew so well. This was almost the old Mykal. This was almost the old feeling. If only this moment could last forever.

Lifting her face, he kissed her lips and she kissed him back.

"Why didn't you tell me from the beginning?" he asked huskily.

"I couldn't." This was going to be the hard part. "We had to be so careful not to upset you in any way."

"But finding out I've got a wife like you wasn't going to upset me," he began. Then he saw the look in her eyes and his face changed. "Or would it?"

She closed her eyes, took a deep breath and sat up on the bed beside him. "It would," she said sadly, "if you knew the whole story."

He looked away for a moment and she wondered what he was thinking. When he looked back, his eyes were troubled. "Maybe we should just leave it alone, Janis," he said quietly. "Maybe it would be better to pretend it never happened—whatever it was."

She shook her head. "We can't do that, Mykal. Even if we wanted to. In fact, now that you are going to be royal, every single fact of your life is going to be common knowledge. You're not going to be able to hide from it."

He groaned and leaned his head back.

"Okay. Lay it on me. What was so horrible that you've felt you had to hide it from me?"

"Okay." She looked at him, all her love in her eyes. This might be the last chance she had to look at him without seeing anger and resentment coming back her way. "When you got blown up on your bike," she began, "we weren't together."

"What happened?"

"Let me start from the beginning."

She filled him in quickly, telling him how they'd met, how they had both been working for military intelligence, both experts at undercover work. "As you used to say, we lived in a world of lies and spies. We had to work hard to keep our own reality apart from that."

His gaze never left her face as she went through their time together, how they had lived and loved, how they had secretly married.

"We were so happy together," she told him earnestly. "We really were so well-matched. It was like a miracle. We could hardly stay away from each other all day."

"Now that I can believe," he said with the hint of a grin.

"But there were a couple of clouds on our horizon. Things you didn't even know about. And it was my fault." Her voice broke.

Reaching out, he took her hand in his, but he didn't say a word.

"Okay, now you know most of the background. But I haven't told you about my brother, Rolo."

"Your brother Rolo." He said it slowly, as though running the name through his memory banks, trying to find the right folder.

"You knew him. He wasn't military but he did some contract work for us and you worked with him a couple of times. He's my baby brother. I basically raised him, as our parents weren't around much." She took a deep breath. How to explain this? "When he was young, I adored him. He was the cutest little boy. He didn't turn out to be what I would have wanted, but I tried." Her voice was shaking, but she couldn't stop now. "And I kept hoping, always hoping, if I could give him just one more chance, maybe this time he would catch on and do well at something. He always needed a break, always had everyone working against him. At least in his mind. You get the picture?"

He nodded, and she noted he was beginning to look a bit distant. That chilled her. But what did she expect?

"We'd been married about two months when he came to me in distress. He was about to be fired once again. He needed evidence to prove he could do the work they were expecting him to do. He had to have something to show them, just one bit of good information. And he wanted me to get it for him."

Mykal winced. "I don't like where this is going," he murmured, eyes hooded.

Her heart sank. He was ready to condemn her without even hearing the whole story. Oh, well. She knew she deserved it.

"I wanted to help him. I wanted to believe him. He's all I have left of my family." She steeled herself, but her words were coming too fast now. She just wanted to get it over with. "In trying to help him, I did something very bad and very stupid. I…I went into your papers and looked for something, anything, something innocuous and simple, something

I could give him to use. Something that you wouldn't even notice."

He was no longer holding her hand. She clenched it into a fist.

"I found the study you had done on the Grieg harbor patterns. You'd said they were useless. So I picked that. I made a copy and I gave it to him."

He was staring at her. "Wow."

She nodded. She knew how bad this was. "I gave him what I'd found, but he called me and said he needed the second page. When I went in to make a copy of that, you walked in and saw me."

"Janis…" His voice was strangled and his eyes were filled with horror and he seemed to be moving as far away from her as he could go.

She closed her eyes for a moment. She didn't want to see that look on his face. She remembered what he had said at the time. "Janis. My God, what have you done? You were my one island of safety and sanity in this crummy world. And now that's gone."

That probably hurt her more than anything

else. To think that she had let him down cut like a knife into her heart.

"I told you this was bad. And it is the reason we aren't together anymore." She took a shaky breath and as she went on, her voice began to sound mechanical. "You could hardly believe what you saw at first. And you told me in no uncertain terms that you could never forgive it. That you could never trust me again. I tried to explain, but of course, it was a stupid explanation anyway and you had every right not to listen to it."

She shook her head, wincing as she remembered that scene. "You were so angry. You felt completely betrayed. You said…" Her voice broke. "You said you never wanted to see me again. I…I ran out of the apartment and I ran and ran. I ran for miles. I finally ended up at Rolo's new apartment, a place you didn't know about. And I stayed with him until the next day." She swallowed hard and went on. "The next day when the secret police came and dragged me away."

He was staring at her. "I don't get it. Why did they do that?"

She shrugged. "Rolo said you'd called them and given information about me, and I…"

"Me?"

"Yes. And I figured he was right. Who else would have done it?"

He shook his head as though he couldn't believe she'd thought that of him. "I thought you said I didn't know where you were."

She shook her head. "Someone must have told you."

He stared at her for a long moment, obviously frustrated that he couldn't remember the facts for himself, and then he said, "I don't believe it."

She shrugged. At this point, she really didn't know what to believe. But she'd been arrested. That much was real. "At any rate, they came. And they took me to the Granvilli prison camp in Swanson, near the border."

He shook his head as though his mind and his heart were too full to say anything.

"I spent two months in that camp. I just got out a few days ago. And I went hunting for you. I heard you'd gone over the border and were living in the city. Someone gave me your address. And I went to your house, still in my prison jumpsuit."

He was staring at her. "Oh, my God, Janis…"

"And there you were, all shot up with shrapnel. And about to be named a prince. So you see, I didn't want to add to your stress level at that moment in time. That's why I didn't tell you."

He closed his eyes and shook his head. Then he looked at her again. "So that wedding ring is ours?"

She half smiled, liking the way he put that, despite everything. "Yes. We only wore them when we were home. We weren't supposed to be married. It was against the military rules." She frowned. "So I don't understand why you were wearing it when your bike hit that IED. Do you?"

He shrugged. "Obviously not."

"And you don't remember what date that was?"

"No."

She glanced at the end of the bed where his chart and other papers were usually posted. There was nothing there.

She looked at him. He looked tired, confused. She reached out and touched his hand, but he made no move to reciprocate. Her throat threatened to swell closed if she didn't get out of here.

"Listen, I've given you a lot to think about," she said, holding back tears. "I'm going to go for now. I'll be back around noon. Okay?"

She looked at him again, wondering if he would tell her not to bother. But he didn't answer. He just stared at her as though he'd never seen her before. She turned and quickly left the room. And once she was in the hall, the tears began to flow. Their marriage was so over.

She walked through the halls, trying to calm herself. There was more to be done. She had to remain competent or things would get even worse. Slowly, bit by bit, she got control again.

A few minutes later she realized she hadn't said anything to him about Kylos showing the house. But that was just as well. She would leave it to Kylos to tell him. He didn't need to hear all the bad news at once.

She hated to leave Mykal all alone like this. She felt as though she was leaving him in the middle of a pack of wolves and expecting him to fend them off all by himself. But she couldn't let herself use that as an excuse to stay longer. She had to leave before it became impossible to go.

And then, as she was passing a group of offices, she saw someone she'd known years before and it occurred to her he might be useful.

"Mr. Dreyfer," she said, approaching the distinguished looking older man. "I don't know if you remember me?"

He smiled and held out his hand. "Of course. You're the Gorgonio girl, aren't you?"

She smiled at him as well, remembering years before when her uncle had tried to engage Mr. Dreyfer as his defense attorney when he'd first been charged with organized crime activities. Mr. Dreyfer had come to the house for extended meetings, but in the end, he'd recommended another attorney.

"Everyone has a right to decent representation," he'd said at the time. "But I can't justify taking a case that won't let me sleep at night. I have a family to consider."

His words had stuck with her and helped

her to make her decision, years later, to try to cut her ties to the Gorgonios.

"Actually, I go by my mother's maiden name, Davos," she told him now.

"Ah. Perhaps that's just as well."

"Yes." She took a deep breath and launched into an explanation of why she was at the castle and what had happened to Mykal. "It's wonderful that he is being given this opportunity," she told him. "But I was thinking he really ought to have representation. It's all so new and unexpected. Would you be interested in talking to him?"

"Yes, of course. It all sounds very exciting and sometimes people get swept away by that. They can often use a bit of wise counsel, which is just what I pride myself in supplying."

"Yes. I trust the people here at the castle and all they're doing, but I think it would be best if he had someone looking after his interests, just to be sure. And since I won't be with him after today…"

"I have some things to wrap up, but I'm at your service. Will tomorrow morning do?"

"I would so appreciate that." She explained

where Mykal was and then left the attorney, feeling satisfied.

She knew what she was doing. She was tying up loose ends after all, just not the ones she'd come seeking to tie up. She'd wanted Mykal to sign their divorce papers. He would probably do that on his own. And she'd wanted him to sign away parental rights. He would never do that. She would have to go and hide where he couldn't find her. But since she wasn't going to be here to help him through all this, she was glad she'd found someone who could do a lot of it for her. One more item off her list.

She still had one of the hardest ones to go. Before she left, he had to know about her family. That might make all this easier for him. Once he wove all that into the background of their relationship tapestry, he would know why she had to go. He would understand.

After all, he was starting on a journey, going somewhere that was beyond her reach. How could she even contemplate going with him when she knew the sort of people she came from? Her uncle—her father's brother— was Max Gorgonio, Ambria's most notorious mobster and the man who had almost ruined Mykal's parents all those years ago. A man who was right now sitting in the royal prison, sentenced to life. His was a name known, feared and despised, all through the country. It was a name she'd been born with. And that was something she could avoid for short periods of time, but ultimately she couldn't run away from.

She stopped into the coffee shop to get an iced mocha drink, and there was Rolo, sitting with her cousin Jasper, both looking glum.

"Janis!" Rolo cried when he saw her. "Thank God. I heard you were here. I've been looking all over for you. We need help."

Her shoulders sagged. Rolo always needed help. This was the first time she'd seen him since the secret police had marched her out of his apartment, and all he could do was ask for help.

She shook her head. "Rolo, I just can't deal with it right now. I need a rest." She saw the shocked expression on his face. He wasn't used to big sister not being there for him. She relented, feeling like a fool. "Oh, why don't you come to my room around three this afternoon. I'll see what I can do." She told him where she was staying and hurried away with her drink. She was going to lie down and think about Mykal. She wouldn't waste one thought on her brother until she had to.

But that only worked for a short time. Eventually she had to think about what Mykal had said about Rolo, and how adamant he'd been that he wouldn't have called out the secret police. She wanted to believe him.

She met Pellea coming out of Mykal's room as she was going in.

"How is he?"

Pellea was beaming. "Tired, but great."

That startled Janis. "Tired? How tired? You don't mean groggy, do you?"

"No, not at all." The queen shrugged. "I assume it's still from the operation."

"Oh. Of course."

Pellea seemed concerned, but she was in a hurry. "I've got a meeting with the ball committee," she said. "You do know there's a royal ball next week?"

"Oh." Too bad she was going to have to miss it.

"Yes. We need to work on a ball gown for you." Pellea laughed. "Originally we thought we were going to be parading a lot of young beauties for Mykal to pick from for his bride. But now I understand that is not an issue."

"Oh." That surprised her. "What did Mykal tell you?"

"Nothing, darling," she said, giving her a hug. "But I can tell by the look on his face when your name is mentioned. We're going to have to have a long talk before we start doing any matchmaking."

Janis pretended she didn't know what the queen was talking about. "As long as he's healthy," she said vaguely, not sure what that meant, but it filled an awkward pause and that was what she used it for. Young beauties? It made her gag to think of it. Still, it was probably good that he begin to think of other women. She was sure the handpicked ladies the crown would bring in for the ball would be perfect in every way. Unlike her.

Pellea went off and Janis went in to see Mykal, steeling herself for the visit. This time, she was going to tell him about her family.

The nurse waved her on through and she went into the room he'd been assigned to.

"Hi," she said, smiling at him lovingly, but not sure what her reception would be.

"Hey." He turned to look at her. For a moment, he didn't smile, as though he was compiling all the new things he knew about her and deciding how to respond. Finally, he smiled back but he seemed sleepy. "You look prettier every time I see you," he said. "I would think just the sight of you should jog my memory back. How could I forget loving you?"

"Amnesia is a tricky thing."

He took her hand in his. "There are so many things I don't know. Where did we live? How long were we married? Did we have a cat?"

She laughed. "No cat. But we did have a lizard that we named Ferdinand. He lived in the courtyard."

He pulled her onto the bed beside him. "Did we live by the ocean? Did we go for long walks in the sand? Did we make love on rainy afternoons?"

"All those things," she said with a sigh,

curling into his embrace. "We were so very happy."

"Until…"

"Yes. Until that awful day."

He held her close, his face buried in her hair. "Forget that day," he murmured. "Leave it behind. Let's go on without it."

She turned and kissed him. "We can't forget it. You heard what I did. You know you'll never feel the same way about me."

He looked pained. "How can I know if I don't feel the same about you when I don't remember how I felt in the first place?"

"When you get your memory back, I think you'll realize…" She took another breath. This was hard to get out. "I think you'll realize that you hate me."

"I hate you?" He shook his head in derision. "Janis, I've felt a lot of things about you since you showed up on my doorstep, but hatred is not one of them."

She sat up, frowning at him. "I don't think you fully understand what I did."

"Yes, I do."

"I betrayed you. It was unforgiveable."

"Yes. And I can't forgive it. But I can understand it. You weren't thinking about me. You were trying desperately to help your younger brother. I'll bet you'd been trying desperately to help him most of your life. You followed a known pattern. It's a pattern you're going to have to work on breaking. But I can understand it."

"Mykal…"

"Enough." He put a finger to her lips to stop her. "Let's put it behind us and go forward."

"We can't. Don't be happy yet. There's more." She steeled herself, ready to begin the tell him about the Gorgonios.

"I don't care," he said. "Come here."

His blue-eyed gaze was mesmerizing. It always had been. She was in his arms and kissing him again, and she knew she wasn't going to tell him about her family. Not yet. This was just too wonderful to forfeit at the moment.

By the time Rolo arrived at her door, she was angry.

"Okay, Rolo. I want the truth," she said as she let him in. "Why did the secret police come for me? Mykal has told me he didn't call them and I believe him."

Rolo looked pained. She could almost see the thoughts going through his head as he tried to decide what part of the truth he should give her.

"Yeah, you're right. See, it was a trap. When I turned over those papers you gave me, they wanted to know where I'd gotten them. I wouldn't tell them."

"And?" she asked coldly.

He threw out his hands as though beseeching pity. "They tortured me, Janis. What could I do?"

"You told them it was me."

"I...yeah, sort of. I couldn't help it. They were torturing me."

"Yeah, I'll bet." She didn't see any marks on him. They'd probably threatened to withhold his video-game-playing time.

"And you told them I was at your apartment."

"No." On this he was adamant. "I wouldn't tell them where you were. Honest."

"Even though they tortured you?" she said sarcastically.

"No, see, what happened was, they followed me back to the apartment. I should have been more careful, I guess."

She remembered that sick, horrible feeling of looking out and seeing that the secret police had surrounded the building.

"Rolo, why didn't you tell Mykal? Why didn't you let him know where I was?"

"Mykal?" He looked surprised. "I thought he was the one you were running from. I didn't think you would want him to know."

She closed her eyes and smiled bitterly. It was a trap, all right. But she was the one who fell into it.

"And anyway, I actually did tell him a couple of days later."

"You did?"

"Yeah. He found out where I lived and he came over and..." He glanced at her furtively. "Well, he sort of made me tell him. He can be a real jerk sometimes."

"And then what did he do?"

He shrugged. "And then he went off to find you and blew up on that motorcycle of his."

Janis closed her eyes and folded her arms over her chest and rocked herself for a moment. He'd been looking for her. All that time she'd been so angry that he hadn't lifted a finger to help her, he'd been looking for her, and then he'd been injured. It wasn't that he hated her. He couldn't help it. She was amazed at how much this changed things. A certain happiness that had died two months before had just sprouted new leaves. He tried to find her. Hallelujah.

She wanted to be alone, wanted to hold this new information to her and revel in it, but her brother was still here and he wouldn't stop talking. She frowned at him, wishing he would go.

"So anyway," he was saying, "all I need is for you to vouch for me. The guard is beginning to ask questions and I know what's coming next. They're going to want to kick me out of here. So if you could just tell the queen I'm okay."

Tell the queen he was okay? Tell her he was her criminally inclined brother, a great example of what could come out of the Gorgonio family. Tell her just to trust him anyway. Yeah, the way she did.

It was hard. She turned and looked at him.

He wasn't a baby anymore but she could see those baby features hidden by the mustache and the unpleasant expression on his face. She was crying inside, crying for the loss of the sweet little boy he'd once been. It was painful.

"No," she said sadly. "Sorry, Rolo. Not this time. The only thing I'll tell the queen is that you're untrustworthy."

He didn't believe her at first. "You…you can't do that to me. We're family."

"We all make choices. You've chosen badly."

"But…"

"I'm choosing to look ahead to a bright and honest future. You would rather look back at a disreputable past and copy it. We're going to have to have a parting of the ways, I'm afraid. You'd better go."

He pleaded for another few minutes, then got angry, but she was adamant. Mykal was a prince here now. She was just as protective of what happened inside these castle walls as anyone.

"Goodbye, Rolo. Maybe we'll meet again some day, but I don't think it will be soon."

He cursed her as he left, but she hardly heard him. She needed to get back to Mykal. She needed to tell him about what he'd done. She also had to tell him about the Gorgonio family before someone else did. Although, if Kylos had been there, she might already be too late.

Mykal lay on his hospital bed, feeling frustrated and impatient. He knew it was going to take some time for recuperation, but he wanted it over with. It was time to get on with his life. He wanted to move.

But right now was not the time. He was exhausted. The physical therapist had arrived about an hour ago and had him up and walking laps in the hallways, no matter how hard he protested. And that was a good thing. He might complain, but he knew getting up and getting back to normal was the best thing he could be doing right now. He didn't want to be babied. He wanted to heal so he could face his future.

But most of all, he wanted to understand his relationship with Janis. Waves of warmth swept through him when he thought of her.

His mind might not remember her, but his heart and soul responded as though nothing was wrong.

He knew as strongly as he knew anything that he wanted her. He wanted her in his life, he wanted her in his bed, he wanted her in his corner. The past was over and gone. No matter what ugliness had come between them, all he had to do was look into her face to know they could overcome anything.

Looking at the IV pumping fluid into his arm, he contemplated yanking the needle out and getting up and going after Janis right now. But that was probably a bad idea. He'd been warned again and again that doing anything of the sort would only make his recuperation last longer, and probably do other damage as well. Besides, a half hour with the physical therapist had totally wiped him out. Trying to go off on his own would probably kill him. He grunted and lay back, angry all over again. He wanted to get out.

But right now, he needed some sleep. Surprisingly, despite his anger, he began to drift off quickly.

He heard a sound at the door and looked up,

hoping to see Janis. But it was Kylos. Disappointment flared, but he nodded a welcome to his brother.

"Hey," he said coolly. "What's happening?"

"Not much." Kylos looked nervous, his gaze jerking about from one part of the room to another as though he were looking for something. "You still don't remember the last two years, right?"

Mykal frowned. "Right. So what?"

"Nothing." He came all the way into the room. "So, how are you feeling?"

"Okay. Hey, I meant to write to Mom and Dad, but I didn't get to it. Can you contact them for me? Can you tell them I love them and want to see them, but that they should stay in Florida until I tell them otherwise? Okay?"

Kylos stared at him for a minute, then jumped as though he'd just realized he was supposed to answer. "Oh. Sure. Listen, I'll take care of that. No problem."

"Good. I wouldn't want them to worry."

"No. Of course not." He grimaced. "Okay, sorry to do this to you, Mykal, but I've got some bad news."

Mykal groaned, not sure he could take any more right now. "You, too?"

"Yeah. I'm afraid you're not going to like it."

He shrugged. "Fire away."

Kylos started, then stopped and fumbled in the pocket of his jacket. "Hey, listen. I forgot." He pulled a little white pill cup out and handed it to his brother, then turned to pour him some water. "The nurse asked me to have you take these. Some kind of vitamins, supposed to make you heal faster."

Distracted by all the confusion, Mykal downed the pills without a second thought. "And the bad news is?" he reminded him.

Kylos grinned, as though he'd suddenly heard good news himself. "Oh, yeah. Your little friend, Janis Davos? That's not her real last name."

Mykal looked at his brother and almost smiled. "No kidding?" he said, expecting to find out Kylos had heard that she was his wife.

"No. I know what her real last name is."

"Marten?"

Kylos looked at him blankly. "Huh? No."

He made a face. "It's Gorgonio. Max Gorgonio is her uncle. She's a Gorgonio. What are the odds, huh? A name our family has hated for fifteen years."

Mykal stared at him. "What?" he said, not really believing it. "Kylos, if you're just trying to pull my chain…"

"No, I swear. Leland, my lawyer, got the goods on her. Andre Gorgonio, Max's brother, was her father. He died when she was a little girl and she was raised in Max's house."

"No."

"I'm just telling you for your own good. I could tell you liked her a lot. So I thought you ought to know. I had my suspicions about her so I had Leland look into it. I'm surprised they didn't pick up on it here at the castle. If they had, they never would have let her in the door."

"No." Mykal was shaking his head, feeling stunned. He couldn't believe it. He didn't want to believe it.

"Funny thing is, Leland knew the family. So when he was here to give me the info this morning, we met in the coffee shop and he identified her right away. She was meeting with her brother Rolo, who I guess is a well-known crook himself." He shrugged. "You never know, do you?"

Mykal didn't respond, and Kylos glanced at his watch. "Hey, gotta go. I'll catch you later." He started off and turned at the door. "Don't feel bad, Mykal. You can see why she's a lying little cheat. She was born to it." And he was gone before Mykal could muster up his sluggish outrage.

And he was outraged. He was enraged at his weakness, enraged at his brother, enraged at Janis. He didn't want to believe it and if it were true he was enraged that it was so. This was just too much. It was as though Janis had purposefully come into his amnesia-damaged life to ruin it further. What the hell!

CHAPTER TEN

JANIS had cleared out her room. Everything she owned was back in her satchel. She was wearing slacks and a jacket that Pellea had given her, but she had no choice. Her blue jumpsuit had disappeared. That was a good thing, she supposed. But she was leaving as lightly as she possibly could.

She had a plan. She put her hand over the slight bulge in her belly and smiled.

"Don't worry, sweet thing," she told her baby silently. "By the time they know we're gone, we'll be on a ferry to the continent. They'll never find us."

No one was manning the nurses' station and she was glad. At some point soon, they would begin denying her entry to places like this. But she had one more lucky chance to see Mykal without interference. She slipped into his room. He was sound asleep, his free arm thrown over his eyes. She stood very still and watched him breathe, loving him so that her throat choked and tears swam into her eyes. It was hard to have to lose him again.

"Mykal." She put a hand on his arm. She needed to tell him goodbye without actually saying it. "Mykal." Bending down, she kissed his lips, then drew back, puzzled. He was sleeping very heavily. She'd never seen him so out of it before. "Mykal." She shook him, beginning to feel a touch of panic, and he moved his arm. His eyes opened slightly.

"What?" he said, slurring the word. He didn't look as though he'd recognized her.

She looked down, stunned. He was drugged.

"Mykal, are you okay?"

"What? Oh, sure. I'm okay." He fought to keep his eyes open, his face contorted in the effort. "Why are you still giving me pain medication?" he asked.

"I'm not."

"Someone is. I can barely keep my eyes open."

"How long have you been like this?"

"I don't know. Come back in about an hour. I should be okay by then." He yawned widely and was back to sleep in no time at all.

She stared down at him for a moment, furious. Turning on her heel, she rushed out to the nurses' station. It was still empty, but the log book was there and she turned it to see who had been in to see him most recently. Her own name was jotted down twice, and Queen Pellea's. King Monte had come by earlier. And the only other name was that of Kylos. He'd been there almost two hours ago.

"Kylos," she breathed, shaking her head as anger surged through her body. It had to be him. But why?

The nurse came in and didn't smile. Janis tried to get her interested in checking Mykal, and she reluctantly agreed to go over his vitals, but at the same time she had a warning for Janis.

"A man from the palace guard came by just a little while ago," she said. "He told me to let him know when you showed up. So I'm going to have to call him."

"Oh." So it had begun. Someone had told the authorities about her and suspicions were beginning to swirl. Her heart sank, but she had expected it. "I wish you wouldn't. I want to come back and check on him in an hour or so to make sure whatever someone gave him is working its way out of his system." Her gaze sharpened. "Did you give him the medication?"

"Me?" She looked horrified. "No. It wasn't me."

"Has any physician been by to see him today?"

"Only the surgeon, but that was early this morning. Oh, and the physical therapist."

"But none of them gave him anything?"

"There's nothing in the notations."

She sighed and glanced at the young woman sideways. Would she call the guard? Maybe yes, maybe no. It would probably be wise not to be here if she did. "Fine," she said at last. "I'll just go then."

She had to leave so as not to be kicked out, but she didn't plan to go far. She found the most inconspicuous seat she could in the waiting area, situated right behind a large fig-leafed plant, where she could keep an eye on both entrances. And there she planned to stay, boiling with anger, until she caught Kylos going in again.

Kylos had been intent on keeping Mykal drugged from the first. She hadn't been able to figure out why exactly, but she was pretty sure it had something to do with his trying to sell the Marten estate without Mykal knowing it was happening. Mykal couldn't defend himself, so she was going to have to do it for him. And so, she sat.

Mykal was moving slow motion in a dream. He could see Janis and hear her, but he couldn't seem to get through to her. It was as though a misty barrier stood between them and no matter how much he waved at her and called to her, she didn't know he was there. She began walking and he ran after her, trying to make his way through the fog to get closer. Every now and then he could reach through and touch her silky hair or catch the hem of her shirt, but that was as close as he could get, and even then, things slipped away. Frustration was building in him. He wanted her to look over and see him but she just kept walking, her head in the clouds.

And then he saw the cliff ahead. She was walking right toward it. She wasn't looking. He ran, he yelled, he threw himself against the misty barrier, but she just kept walking toward the abyss. Closer and closer. His breath burned in his throat from trying so hard to reach her. She was going to go over. One more step…

"No!" he screamed.

But she went over the edge of the cliff. Certain death!

But then he remembered—he could fly! He could still save her. All he had to do was jump after her and use his flying powers. He ran as hard as he could for the edge and leaped over. He could see her plummeting toward the rocks below. He spread out his arms and arched his back to fly. But it didn't happen. He'd forgotten how to do it. Below, she hit the rocks. In a moment, he would, too. It was the end. No more happiness. Just…nothing.

It was after ten when Kylos finally showed up. Only a few stragglers were left in the halls. The coffee shop had closed. Most people on this floor had gone to their rooms.

Janis heard him coming down the hall and shrank back even farther behind the plant that hid her from view. And there he was, looking furtively to right and left before ducking into the medical center. The moment he vanished into the offices, she jumped up and followed him.

Anger at Mykal's brother threatened to surge in her but she forced it back. She didn't want anything to shake her concentration from the job at hand. She was certain he was the one drugging Mykal, and she was determined to catch him in the act and stop him cold.

Once again there was no one manning the nurses' station and she made a mental note to file a complaint against the lax security situation. But she couldn't think about that now. Kylos had just disappeared into Mykal's room and she had to stay focused. Stepping quietly up to the door, she stopped and listened to what was going on inside.

"Hey, buddy," Kylos was saying. "How are you feeling?"

"What's going on?" Mykal's voice was

bleary, startled. It was obvious he was mostly still asleep.

"Not a thing. Take it easy. I'm glad you're still groggy. That'll keep you quiet for a while."

"What? I don't get it."

"No problem. Just stay cool."

"Where's Janis?"

"Janis? She's gone. No one knows where she is."

"What?"

"Listen, the nurse gave me a couple more of those vitamins she wants you to take. Let me get you a cup of water. Okay, here you go…."

Janis thrust the door open, rage consuming her. "Drop the pills, Kylos. And get your hands off my husband."

"Your what?" He stared at her, thunderstruck.

"Do what I say. Now." She'd trained for months to give her voice this sort of authority and it was coming in handy now. Kylos looked downright terrified. "And give me those pills." She grabbed them out of his hand while he was still off balance, glaring at him. "How could you do this?"

She leaned over Mykal and pressed the nurse's call button. Glancing at him, she saw that his eyes were closed. Could he possibly be asleep again with all this going on?

"You don't know what you're talking about," Kylos said, but he was backing toward the door. Then he stopped and a crafty look came over his face. "You may think Mykal is your husband," he said. "But that won't last long. I told him about your background, that you were a Gorgonio. He pretty much came right out and said that was the last straw as far as he was concerned."

She looked down at Mykal, telling herself to ignore what Kylos was saying. He was obviously using any weapon he could think of to shake her. But at the same time, she knew Mykal's reaction to her background would not be good. And that was why she was leaving.

"Come on, Janis. You know the royal family will never accept a Gorgonio." He shook his head. "Game over, baby." He gave her an evil grin. For some strange reason he didn't seem to be anxious to get out of the room any longer.

The nurse came in and looked at them all, wide-eyed. "What is going on in here?" she demanded.

"Hey," Kylos said quickly. "I just caught her trying to give my brother those pills she's got in her hand. I think she should be arrested."

Janis turned to the nurse, never dreaming she might believe him. "Actually, it's the other way around," she said calmly. "I caught him trying to drug Mykal. Please call the castle guard."

The nurse looked from one to the other, put her mobile to her ear and called the guard.

"Someone's lying and I don't know which one of you it is," she said testily. "But you," she said, pointing to Janis, "are the one the guard was looking for earlier, aren't you? And the patient is his brother. So I guess I'm going to have to take his word for it."

"What?" Janis realized, to her horror, that Kylos might just get away with drugging Mykal. And not just that, he was going to have free rein to do it again. "No, you can't believe him."

"You're the one with a record, babe," Kylos said with a grin. "We know all about you now. Did a little time in prison camp, didn't you?"

"On the Granvilli side."

He shrugged. "Once a con, always a con, that's what they say, don't they?"

"Please listen to me," she said to the nurse, desperate now. "I was not the one doing this. You may not believe me. Okay. But please, please, make sure there is better security so he can't do this again. You've got to put a guard on Mykal. Please."

The castle guard had arrived, eyes beaming as he saw Janis. "We've been looking for you, lady. You've got some questions to answer."

"I'll answer anything you want. I'll go anywhere you want and do anything you want. But please, please, just put a guard on Mykal. And don't let his brother get anywhere near him."

No one gave her any promises. She could only hope for common sense to rule. Two guards marched her through the halls to the little old-fashioned jail cell they kept for situations like this. She was thinking that this couldn't be happening, that it was a nightmare scenario, and yet, she'd been through it before. So it could happen. And it was.

There they were again—the bars. The clang of metal on metal. The scrape of the key in the lock. She was back, but for how long?

She sighed as she settled in. At least she'd alerted them to Kylos. That was the most she could do at this point. If she could just talk to Pellea…

"Can you ask the queen to call me?" she asked her young, gum-chewing jailer.

"Are you kidding? At this time of night?" But he relented a bit. "Listen, here's a pen and paper. Write her a note. I'll make sure her maid gets it in the morning."

And that was the most she could do. Her first goal was to make sure that Mykal was safe. And her second was to get out of the castle before Pellea realized she was pregnant. Once the royal family knew that, and knew she and Mykal were married, they would never let her go. Even if they would scorn to make her royal, they would certainly want her baby to be one of them.

Royal—hah! Here she was with a cot for a bed, one thin blanket and nothing much else. She'd left her satchel with all her worldly possessions in Mykal's hospital room. So she had nothing with her. It would be a long night.

Janis got a plate of soggy scrambled eggs in the morning, and then Pellea arrived.

"What on earth is going on?" she asked sharply.

Janis looked up and the first thing she noticed was the queen's demeanor. Her eyes were lacking the usual warmth and affection she was known for. She was holding back a bit, staying well out of reach beyond the bars.

"Please explain this to me."

Janis rose and faced her resolutely, trying to explain. She told her about her suspicions of Kylos and his motives. She described finding Mykal's parents' death certificates though Kylos refused to tell the truth about them while he seemingly tried to sell the house, about how he'd been pushing to keep Mykal drugged from the first, so that he couldn't ask any questions or really get his mind around what his brother might be doing.

"When I realized that he was drugging Mykal again, I had to do something. I watched him go in and I caught him at it."

Pellea's gaze hadn't warmed a bit. "Only he says he caught you."

"Yes. That's not true." She looked at Pellea, wishing she knew a way to convince her. "Your Majesty, I know you are caught in the middle."

"Tell me this." Now her eyes were cold as winter ice. "Is it true that Max Gorgonio is your uncle?"

Her heart sank. This was the coup de grâce, wasn't it? This was the one thing she couldn't explain away. "Yes," she said in the soft voice of a lost one.

"Is it true that you were raised in his house along with his family?"

"Yes." Gathering all her nerve, she raised her gaze to meet Pellea's and try to get her to understand. "But that has nothing to do with this."

Pellea raised a hand to stop her. "I'm sorry, Janis. I can't just take your word for it. I should never have let you stay in the first place. It's my fault."

Janis choked and her eyes stung. "I…I'm sorry."

Pellea didn't smile. "I'll have to look into this further," she said. "Take care. I'll send you word on how things are going."

Janis watched as she left through the heavy steel door. Once it clanged into place, leaving her all alone again, her tears began to flow.

The next stop for Pellea was Mykal's room. He was still asleep when she entered, but she got a washcloth dripping with cold water and applied it to his face. That did the trick and he was soon sitting up, squinting at her.

"Arrgghh," he said.

"And well you might," Pellea said. "You look like hell."

He groaned again and tried to widen his eyes. "I feel like I have a very bad hangover. Either that or someone used me for shark bait during the night. What happened?"

"That's what I'm here to find out."

He closed his eyes, letting his head fall

back. "Okay. Let me know when you come up with an answer," he muttered.

"Mykal, listen to me. Someone drugged you yesterday. The nurse has run some tests and it seems to be true. Who could have done it?"

He tried to think but his brain wasn't really ready for that yet. "I don't know. The doctor?"

"No." She looked at him impatiently. "You had a number of visitors, including Janis and your brother. Would either one of them have wanted you out cold for any reason?"

He tried harder, but all he got was static. "No. I don't get it."

Pellea sighed. "All right. I'll come back later when you're feeling a bit more alert. But remember. We're trying to pull all the threads together on a few different stories of what might have happened. I'll let you know as soon as we have all the facts." She patted him and turned to go. "You just get some sleep and rest up."

He groaned. Getting sleep and resting up were all he ever did anymore. He was sick of it. But he closed his eyes and the next thing he knew, it was two hours later and an attorney was sitting in the chair beside his bed, going through papers and telling him things he didn't really understand.

Mykal stared at the attorney, Mr. Dreyfer, who had just said Janis had sent him.

"Why? Are you sure it was Janis?"

"Yes, I'm sure. She thought you needed representation. Someone to be on your side."

Mykal stared at the wall, trying to figure this out. "She's leaving, isn't she?" he said softly.

"I believe she said she had business to take care of."

"No." His voice was rough and adamant. "She should be here taking care of my business. But she sent you to do it instead." He frowned. "Not a good sign."

"Janis is a wonderful young woman, but I don't believe she has the legal background to understand."

"Of course not. But she understands us and what we need better than you could ever do." He shook his head and stared at the wall again. "No offense. But Janis is my wife and I'm afraid she just walked out in order to make things easier for me."

The attorney left, saying he would be back again tomorrow when Mykal's life had calmed down a bit. Mykal stared at the wall until the nurse came in to check his bandages.

"Hello, nurse," he said, looking at her in a friendly manner. "Is the sun shining outside?"

"I'm sorry, sir, I have no way of knowing. We're in a castle, you know. We don't see the outside all that well most of the time."

"Oh. Sorry. I didn't know."

She worked on him for a few more minutes and then pulled back as though finished with the job. He frowned at her thoughtfully. Just beyond her, he saw Janis's satchel shoved into the corner. She must have left it here. But when?

That meant that she was still here in the castle, didn't it? She hadn't gone off and left him. Not yet. Maybe, if he could gather his strength, he could find a way to go after her. He would have to think about it.

"Nurse, could you tell me if Janis has been by today?"

The nurse's face changed dramatically. "Uh…no, sir. I thought you knew. She was caught last night."

That hit him like a thunderbolt. He stared at her, appalled. "Caught? Doing what?"

The nurse's eyes got very big. "From what I heard, she was trying to drug you with pills, sir."

"What?" How absurd. Utterly ridiculous. She had to be joking. "What?"

"Your brother caught her doing it." She looked very satisfied. "But don't you worry, she's in the castle jail, waiting for justice to be served." She smiled at him. "In the meantime, we're on orders to make sure no one comes in this room without a witness."

Janis, drugging him? No. Someone was making that up. Janis would never do anything like that. She had her moments. Like when he caught her stealing his work to give to her brother. But other than that, what had she ever done to make him angry? Nothing.

He closed his eyes and remembered things—Janis in a bikini, jumping off the side of the pool into the silver water. Janis cooking pizza and catching the ancient old stove in their apartment on fire. Janis, in his arms, making him think an angel was making love to him, a very sexy angel with breasts just made for his hands and skin like buttered honey....

His eyes shot open. He had his memory back.

"Nurse!" he called as he ripped out the needle to his IV. "I've got to get out of here."

He looked down, glad to see he had on pajama bottoms and not some diminutive hospital gown. No pajama top, but that hardly mattered. No shoes. No time to find some.

"Sir!" The nurse had come in and was trying to stop him. "What are you doing? You can't go out like that."

"Oh, yeah? Watch me."

A doctor came into the hall, trying to stop him as well.

"Sir, think of your position. You're about to be named a prince. You can't do this."

"I have to do this." As gently as he could, he moved the physician out of his way. "Now tell me how to get to the castle jail."

A moment for directions and he was off. He wanted to run but he was pretty sure things were still too newly patched together to take the jostling. But he walked very fast and could tell by the reaction coming from everyone he passed that he made quite a spectacle with his bare, muscular chest glistening in the artificial light of the castle halls. But he didn't care. He had to get to Janis before she spent another minute in that place.

He burst through the jail doors and looked into a pair of startled faces as the jailors realized who he was.

"I've come to get my wife," he told them. "Give me the key."

"Uh, I'm afraid we can't."

"Now," he roared, and then he followed the inevitable glance they each made toward where the key was hung and got it for himself. Next, he was marching down the hall to the cell where she was standing at the bars, wondering what all the commotion was about.

"Mykal!" she cried when she saw him. "What are you doing? You're going to hurt yourself." But she was half laughing as she took in his casual attire.

"I'm coming to get my woman," he told her.

"You can't do this," she protested happily. He stood there before her in all his glory, the pajama bottoms riding low on his beautiful hips, the muscles rippling in his arms and chest, and she nearly swooned.

"Really?" he said as he turned the key in the lock. "What the hell good is it being royal if I can't even rescue my own wife from the castle jail?" He opened his arms to her. "Come on," he said. "Let's go."

She flew into his arms and held him close. "You don't think I was drugging you, do you?" she asked as he buried his face in her hair.

"Of course not," he said. "And even if you were, I'd know it was for a good reason."

That made her laugh again. He swept her out of the jail and out into the halls again. She was vaguely aware that Pellea was there, calling out directions to them, but she was too busy holding on to Mykal to pay attention. And then she found herself in Pellea's garden and Mykal was kissing her just the way he used to. Birds were chirping. The waterfalls were sending music through the area. The scent of roses filled the air.

"Isn't this Pellea's room?" she asked.

"Yes. You wait here. I've got to make a few phone calls."

She sighed and closed her eyes, settling into the sumptuous couch. Just moments before, she'd been lying on a thin cot in a jail cell, and now she was in the queen's private suite. Mykal had ridden to the rescue this time. The winds of fate blew erratically, didn't they? As long as they blew true in the end, it didn't matter.

Mykal was back, still looking gorgeous in his pajama bottoms. He sank into the couch beside her.

"Pellea said for us to make ourselves at home," he told her as he took her into his arms. "She knows we need some time to talk and she won't be back for hours."

"Hours," she breathed, rubbing her face against his chest. "Hours to hold on to each other. Heaven." She peeked up at his face. "So you know it was Kylos who was drugging you?"

"Yes. And I think I might know why. My memory seems to be back."

"Oh!" She looked up into his face and laughed. "Now do you see? Do you remember what is was like when we were together?"

He nodded, smiling at her.

Her own smile faded. "Do you remember what I did?"

"You already told me all about that." He pulled her close again. "I remember everything," he told her, his voice low and husky. "I've got you back, now and in the past, and this time, I'll never let you go."

He kissed her and she melted into him, all heat and tenderness.

"Wait," she said, struggling to come back to the surface and get a few things settled before they gave themselves up to pure passion and pleasure. "You said you thought you knew why Kylos was drugging you?"

"Janis, I've got my memory back. I knew about my parents dying in the accident before I even met you. I also knew their will gave everything to me to handle as I saw fit. But when I showed up injured, with no memory, Kylos and his lawyer friend, Leland, thought they saw their chance. They tampered with the will and were trying to sell the estate before I came back to normal and could stop them. The longer I was under sedation, the better chance they had of getting it done and taking off with the money."

"Your own brother!"

"Yes. I guess we all get saddled with family members we'd rather not have to deal with," he said significantly.

She looked into his eyes. He must know about her ties to the Gorgonios, even though she hadn't had the nerve to tell him. And he understood. How had she gotten so lucky? She sighed and nodded. "What's going to happen to them?" she asked.

"I'm afraid they will both be prosecuted for their crimes. I only hope that Kylos finally learns his lesson." He kissed her nose. "But enough about him. I have something I have to explain to you. I'm sure you wondered, all that time you were in the camp, why I didn't do something about getting you out."

She drew in a shaky breath. "Actually, I did wonder at the time."

"Of course. That was an awful day. I was so angry with you and I said some awful things. And regretted them almost immediately. But you were gone. I couldn't find you anywhere. I nearly went crazy. I looked for you everywhere and no one knew where you'd gone. For days I searched and searched.

I couldn't find your brother, I couldn't find any of your coworkers. Finally someone told me where Rolo's new apartment was and I went over right away. He told me that he'd seen you being carted off by the secret police. It looked like you were going in the direction of the prison camp. So I put on my wedding ring and fired up my trusty old motorcycle and raced out there."

Janis reveled in happiness. This was exactly what she would have expected him to do. But she had a question. "Why the wedding ring?" she asked.

He smiled and hugged her close. "I wanted to show you that my commitment to you was stronger than my work, my patriotism, than anything else in the world. It was just you. You are all that matters to me. And we're going to be together through all this royalty nonsense. Nothing is going to tear us apart again."

She shook her head, still worried. She just didn't see how it could work. "Mykal, don't you understand? There are just too many things against us."

He pulled her up where he could look into her face. "Like what?"

"My betrayal, which is something you can say you'll push aside, but you know it will always be there. Then there's my time in prison camp. How many royals have been there? There's the problem of my birth into the most notorious crime family in the nation. There's the fact that my family almost ruined your adoptive parents. How could anyone accept that you might want me after all that?"

He shook his head, mocking her. "And then there's the baby."

She made a worried face. "Oh, yeah. The baby."

He smiled down at her, covering her tiny belly with his big, wide hand. "I can't give up my baby."

"But, if the royal family won't accept me, I'm afraid they'll still want the baby and I can't leave the baby with you."

"No, Janis." He smiled at her. "You're getting all confused. You won't leave the baby with me, because I won't be here, either. If you can't stay, I can't stay. I go where you go."

He was ready to give up a place in the castle for her. She could see it in his face. She loved him more than anything and she was beginning to believe they just might be able to do this thing.

"Oh, Mykal. Are you sure?"

"If this royal family can't accept me with a wife like you, they can't have me. It's simple as that."

She threw her arms around his neck and clung to him. "I love you so."

He winced. He still had those wounds on his back. But he didn't let her see it. Right now, he wanted her happiness more than anything else.

"That goes double for me," he said huskily and he drew her closer. "Because I've got two of you to love."

* * * * *

LARGER-PRINT BOOKS!

GET 2 FREE LARGER-PRINT NOVELS PLUS
2 FREE GIFTS!

◊ Harlequin®

Romance

From the Heart, For the Heart